"I'm bringing my daughter to Texas to live with me.

I'm all she's got, and really, I'm glad. I want to claim her as my daughter."

Kate thought that was admirable. Many men would have tried their best to get out of the responsibility of raising an eight-year-old. "This will really change your life."

"Exactly!" Travis said, straightening and, in the process, moving a little closer. "I've never thought about children much. I've never been around them, since I'm an only child and most of my friends are single. So I'm going to need some help. Your help."

Kate knew her surprise showed on her face. "*My* help? What are you talking about?"

Dear Reader,

With mixed emotions I have written the last Harlequin American Romance novel set in Ranger Springs, Texas. I really love these characters and wanted to tell the story of two people who start over in the Hill Country, finding more than they anticipated. I also love the town of Ranger Springs, the people who "live" there, and other stories I have written about them. So although there won't be new stories, I hope you will revisit the friends and families who found their perfect match and began a new life in this friendly town. The Fourth of July committee, which has been planning throughout seven books, finally got their parade!

Kate Wooten, sister of Travis Whitaker from *Coming Home to Texas,* is now divorced and starting over with her six-year-old son. She's a schoolteacher and former soccer mom—not the kind of woman "retired" stuntman and animal trainer Luke Simon is interested in. That is, until he needs someone to give him lessons on how to be a daddy to his newly discovered eight-year-old daughter. Kate is the perfect teacher for this job, but he soon realizes he can't keep their relationship professional. Kate must decide if she will risk her heart one more time for the right man, to create a new family.

As you read *Daddy Lessons,* I hope you will consider the plight of unwanted animals, whether they are the retired performance animals that Luke cares for or the thousands of pets in shelters or on the streets. I give special thanks to D. J. Schubert of the Black Beauty Ranch, run by The Fund for Animals in Murchison, Texas. What a wonderful sanctuary and what a giving man, who answered all my questions.

Best wishes to everyone, and happy reading.

Victoria Chancellor

Daddy Lessons

VICTORIA CHANCELLOR

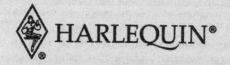

HARLEQUIN®

TORONTO • NEW YORK • LONDON
AMSTERDAM • PARIS • SYDNEY • HAMBURG
STOCKHOLM • ATHENS • TOKYO • MILAN • MADRID
PRAGUE • WARSAW • BUDAPEST • AUCKLAND

ISBN 0-373-75102-8

DADDY LESSONS

Copyright © 2006 by Victoria Chancellor Huffstutler.

In loving memory of my mother-in-law, Lillian Huffstutler,
1919-2005, who supported and loved me like a daughter.
We miss you so much, Sudie.

Books by Victoria Chancellor

HARLEQUIN AMERICAN ROMANCE

844—THE BACHELOR PROJECT
884—THE BEST BLIND DATE IN TEXAS
955—THE PRINCE'S COWBOY DOUBLE
959—THE PRINCE'S TEXAS BRIDE
992—THE C.E.O. & THE COOKIE QUEEN
1035—COMING HOME TO TEXAS

Don't miss any of our special offers. Write to us at the
following address for information on our newest releases.

Harlequin Reader Service
U.S.: 3010 Walden Ave., P.O. Box 1325, Buffalo, NY 14269
Canadian: P.O. Box 609, Fort Erie, Ont. L2A 5X3

Prologue

Kate loved sharing a meal with her son Eddie, her brother Travis and his family at the Four Square Café. The decor was a little outdated, even by the current retro standards, the menu a bit heavy on carbs, sugar and fats, and the service not nearly as speedy as the fast-food place on the highway. But the waitresses were friendly, the food delicious and the company the best she'd had in years.

Since about six months into her marriage with her lying, cheating ex-husband Ed, to be exact.

"Here you go," Charlene Jacks said as she delivered a tray of burgers and fries to the table.

"Thanks, Charlene," Travis said. He handed a plate to his wife Jodie, which she immediately passed to Eddie.

"Thank you, Aunt Jodie."

Kate smiled at her six-year-old son, the light of her life, who'd thankfully remembered his manners. Her divorce and Ed's subsequent desertion had been especially hard on their son—not that Ed had ever been an involved parent. He'd never been the kind of father that Travis was already with his infant daughter, Marsha.

"Earth to Kate," Travis said, interrupting her thoughts in the same way he had when they were children. He held out her plate. "If you're not hungry…"

"Oh, no you don't. I'll take that right now." When she'd lived the suburban lifestyle, she'd enjoyed all the trendy chain restaurants. Now she was happy with simpler fare…even if she did sometimes miss a good grilled chicken caesar salad.

"You folks need anything else?" Charlene asked.

"We're great, thanks," Travis said, and Kate smiled up at her while Jodie adjusted Marsha's pacifier.

As Charlene moved away from the table, the sunlight flooding through the front window of the café made Kate squint. And then she noticed something that made her eyes open wide. Something she hadn't seen in Ranger Springs in the two months she'd lived here.

The heavy blub-blub-blub of the motorcycle engine died as the bike came to a stop across the street, facing the gazebo in the middle of the town square. With the rider's back to her, she worked her gaze up from his heavy boots to his faded, tight jeans, past the black leather jacket to the dark, too-long hair that blew in the cool breeze.

He threw his muscular leg over the seat and stepped away from the bike. Kate caught her breath. Wow.

"Kate! Do you want your lunch or not?"

She blinked, moving her focus from the scene outside the window to Travis. "Yes, I want...lunch," she said in a slightly shaky voice. She absolutely did not want to stare at the bona-fide bad boy on the big motorcycle.

"Are you okay?" Jodie asked, placing a hand on Kate's forearm.

"I'm fine. I just saw...I wonder who that is. He doesn't exactly look like a local."

"Who?"

Jodie and Travis both turned toward the window. Travis narrowed his eyes, a sure sign he was getting all protective. "No, he's not local."

"Like I would have missed *him*," Jodie added, then smiled at Travis's deepening frown.

Kate grinned. She loved the way her brother and sister-in-law teased each other, argued in a good-natured way and made up with lots of love. She and Ed—the lying, cheating rat—had never developed that type of relationship.

"Who, Mommy?" Eddie asked.

"Just some man on a motorcycle," Kate replied casually, then looked back out the window. The man who'd just breezed into town didn't resemble the local guys at all. They wore snap-front Western shirts, the softer, looser jeans made for riding horses, not Harleys, and cowboy or work boots. They definitely didn't look like...that.

The man was walking toward the restaurant, as

though he'd sensed her ogling him. Not that she was exactly ogling. She was a thirty-two-year-old divorced mother without a steady job or a permanent place to live. She owned a few pieces of furniture, a couple of suitcases of clothes and a few boxes of personal belongings. Until she found a job, hopefully teaching school, she was officially unemployed, although she did substitute teach whenever possible. She didn't have the luxury of ogling strange men.

Still, her heart thumped as he opened the door of the café. The bell overhead tinkled, drawing the attention of everyone in the place. He brought in the crisp winter air and the smell of well-worn leather. Or perhaps she just imagined the leather. One thing she wasn't imagining was her shocking appreciation for a one-hundred-percent male. No, make that one-hundred-percent *off-limit* male.

"Hey, Luke," Hank McCauley called out from across the room. From the corner of her eye, Kate saw him rise from his booth and head toward the biker.

"Hank." The man's soft, deep voice fit his persona as well as his white T-shirt molded his pecs and abs. He walked right by them but didn't look over. Didn't politely smile or nod as most of the locals did. Didn't even notice she'd been practically drooling, despite her mental efforts to curb her unexpected reaction.

The last thing she needed right now was an attraction to a man. She didn't have the time, energy or confidence to start a relationship. And then there was

Eddie. She needed to be both mother and father to him now that Ed was out of the picture. Now that their lives had been turned upside down.

"Your hamburger's getting cold, sis," Travis said in a warning tone.

Just then Charlene approached their table and mentioned, as she refilled their iced tea, "He's Hank's friend from California. Hank said he'd be in sometime around noon. Rode all the way to Texas on his Harley."

"California?" Jodie asked. "I wonder where. I'll have to find out."

"It's a big state," Travis said in a slightly peeved tone. "Just because you're from the same state doesn't mean he's your new best friend."

"Jealous, darling?" she teased.

Travis snorted. "Of him? Hardly."

"I think he's a very attractive man," Charlene added. "Not for me, of course. I mean in general. He looks like a movie star, but Hank said he's a stunt-man and a trainer."

Personal or animal?

"Wow, a stuntman," Eddie said. "I know what they do."

Oh, great. Looked as though she was going to have a serious case of hero worship. That, combined with her own wandering thoughts, meant they'd *all* better avoid the newcomer. "I'm sure he's just taking a short vacation." *Probably a vacation from all the gorgeous Hollywood women chasing after him.*

"According to Hank, he's bought 640 acres, an old ranch just out of town," Charlene said, then grinned. "Travis, he's your new neighbor!"

Neighbor? That would be bad. Very, very bad. Kate swallowed the lump in her throat with a big drink of iced tea, vowing to have a long talk with Eddie when they got home about how they needed to not bother their new neighbor, at least until he had time to get settled in. And they knew more about him. By then, maybe she could be objective. Maybe she'd even convince herself that she could tell a good guy from a bad one without spending years being married to him.

Eddie swiveled in his chair and watched the newcomer with way too much interest. Yes, she and Eddie both needed to stay away from their new neighbor. She only hoped she could follow her own advice.

Chapter One

Luke leaned against the sturdy new fence that defined the pasture for Lola and Lollipop, two cantankerous zebras; Spot and Potsy, two arthritic Shetland ponies; and Gordon the ill-tempered donkey. Beneath a row of hackberry trees near the driveway, two swayback snowy white horses stood side by side, lazily swishing their tails in unison.

He'd moved to this small town in the Texas Hill Country for just this reason—an affordable place with a good climate where he could provide a "retirement" home for unwanted animals. Where they—and he—could live in peace and quiet. Land in California had been too expensive. So he'd come back to Texas, to the town where his friend Hank McCauley lived, even though this particular place wasn't Luke's hometown, not that he thought of any particular place as home.

Besides, he didn't need a hometown. He was a grown man who could take care of himself. These animals didn't have anywhere to go except a slaughter-house or rendering plant.

The sound of barking reminded him that he should feed the Jack Russell terriers in their run near the barn. But first he needed to make sure his inquisitive little neighbor got back through the fence—the one that divided his property from Travis Whitaker's ranch.

Ever since the animals had begun arriving from California, Oklahoma and Colorado, Eddie Wooten had started visiting Luke's property. He hid behind the newly painted barn, lurked behind shrubby Mesquite trees and sneaked between the hackberry trees in the fencerow. When he figured Luke wasn't looking, he'd coax the animals to him with carrots and apples. The same scenario had occurred at least a half-dozen times, enough that Luke was now on the lookout for one little boy.

If Eddie stayed on his side of the fence, Luke wouldn't worry. But the boy was fearless when it came to animals—especially Lola and Lollipop—and put himself in danger by walking into the pasture. Eddie could be accidentally bitten, stepped on or knocked down.

He tried to remember himself as a child, but the image wouldn't form. Sometimes he thought he'd been born at age fourteen. Had he ever been as inquisitive as Eddie? As naive?

Luke winced at the memory of Kate Wooten arriving at his ranch the last time the boy had strayed over. She'd been tense and worried and yet more beautiful than he remembered from the first time he'd seen her. She'd held Eddie to her briefly, assured herself that he was uninjured, and then soundly chastised him for running off. She'd told him that he absolutely could not come here again, that he had to stay away from the animals. Then she'd turned those wide gray eyes on Luke and apologized for her son's impulsive, inappropriate behavior.

He'd never heard childish curiosity called "inappropriate" behavior before. Only later had he discovered, through an innocent conversation with Gwendolyn McCauley at the local café, that Kate was an elementary school teacher. She was one classy lady, and obviously well educated. Her reserved attitude and the fact that she stuck around only long enough to retrieve her son made their differences real obvious.

He'd gruffly told her that her son should stay on his side of the fence because any animal could be dangerous, even one that looked perfectly harmless. She'd looked at him in horror for an endless moment, then bundled off Eddie without another word. Luke had barely seen her since. Certainly hadn't spoken to her.

She apparently found him even more frightening than his animals.

Eddie cleared the fence and ran in the direction of the Whitaker house. Or more specifically, the Whitaker garage, where he lived in the apartment upstairs with his mother.

Luke didn't want to dwell on the attractive but uptight sister of his coolly polite neighbor. Travis wasn't hostile, but he seemed suspicious of Luke and the Last Chance Ranch. It really didn't matter because Luke owned the land and was here to stay, regardless of what the locals thought or said.

Just as he turned away to walk back to the house, a truck pulled off the rural road into the long driveway, past his house to the large barn. His feed shipment had arrived. When the driver, a young man named Lester Boggs, stopped and rolled down the window, Luke told him, "Pull on around to the barn door. I'll help you unload."

"You runnin' some kind of zoo?" Lester asked as they piled up the sacks of feed.

"Not exactly."

"Aunt Joyce said Hank told her and Thelma you used to work in Hollywood."

"I did a little animal training. A little stunt work."

"You ever do any stunts for Ben Affleck?"

"Not that I can remember."

"Johnny Depp?"

"Not really."

The other man seemed disappointed. Well, too bad. Luke didn't believe in living his life in public. Hank had warned him people would be curious about any newcomer. A newcomer with a menagerie of animals…that caused extra speculation. Luke didn't care, as long as he wasn't bothered.

The previous owner hadn't taken good care of the

ranch. All the animals except a few half-wild barn cats had been sold long ago. The place was as close to deserted as Luke had ever seen. His first priorities had been the barn and fences. Everything else could wait.

"Why would you want a bunch of old animals?" Lester asked as they worked on the hay bales. Next year Luke planned to grow his own crop of coastal Bermuda, but for now he needed to buy hay locally.

"I like them," Luke said, hooking another bale. "They spent their lives performing in circuses, films, animal acts. They've earned a retirement, but some of them were going to be put down because they weren't useful anymore. He felt his anger build at the injustice. "Some were wasting away without food or shelter. I'm giving them a home for as long as they live."

Lester looked at him as though he were nuts. "Whatever you say, Mr. Simon," he said cautiously.

Luke didn't respond. He'd had no intention of talking about himself to strangers. And as far as he was concerned, almost everyone here was a stranger, even if he did know their names and where they lived. Even if they were neighbors.

KATE STOPPED LOADING the washing machine when she saw the telltale burrs on her son's fleece pullover. "Oh, Eddie." He'd been in the pasture where he'd been forbidden to venture.

"Hey, Kate," Jodie, looking gorgeous in a coral athletic suit, said from the doorway of the downstairs laundry room. Jodie, a plus-size model who had a clothing line and a fragrance, and Travis had been married for almost a year. Their daughter was just beginning to teethe—still far too young to be slipping away on her own to get into trouble.

"Hi, Jodie," Kate replied, trying to coax some enthusiasm into her voice.

"What's wrong?"

"My son. Our neighbor. Everything."

"Surely it's not that bad," Jodie said sympathetically, leaning her hip against the dryer.

Kate held the garment briefly to her chest. "I'm frustrated that I can't stop Eddie from running over to our neighbor's ranch to see those odd animals. He could be injured by Travis's huge longhorn cattle along the way. He could fall and hurt himself—hit his head on a rock or break his leg. And how would anyone know?"

"Would you feel better if Travis moved the cattle for now? Or would you like to find someplace else to live? You know Travis offered to rent you a house closer to the school."

"No, I don't want to put him out any more than I already have."

"It's no trouble."

"That's nice of you to say, but giving me free rent and worrying along with me over Eddie's excursions across the fence are enough for now. Besides, I'll be on my feet soon. I hope."

Jodie came over and gave her a hug. Kate felt like throwing her arms around her sister-in-law and sobbing into her shoulder. But she wouldn't. Jodie was too kindhearted, and Kate knew her melancholy was temporary. Or at least she hoped it was.

She pulled back and sniffed. "I'm sorry. I'm just down right now. I...I'm obviously not doing something right. Sometimes, especially when I spend a little too much time alone thinking, I wonder if I'm doing *anything* right."

"Of course you are! We all love you. And Eddie is a great kid, even if he is a little too adventurous at times."

"He *is* a great kid, but I wonder how much is my doing. I mean, I married the wrong man, allowed him to take care of me financially if not emotionally, and closed my eyes to both his unscrupulous investment decisions and his philandering. I've never worked outside the home, never even considered that I needed credit in my own name. I was blind and dumb to my lying, cheating husband until everything in my 'perfect' world came tumbling down."

"You're being way too hard on yourself."

Kate shook her head. "It's all true. And now I'm responsible for everything—Eddie's health and welfare, his education and development. I need to run a household on almost no money, because about all I can do is substitute teach until I get a permanent job." Kate sniffed again. "I'm sorry, Jodie. I'm just having a little pity party down here in the laundry room. I didn't mean to burden you."

"We keep telling you it's no burden. We love you,

Kate. We've never used the garage apartment, so you're welcome to stay as long as you'd like, until you and Eddie get tired of us and *want* to move away."

Kate attempted a shaky smile. "You're too nice."

In a moment of brash confidence, she'd decided not to take any more handouts from her oil-wealthy father and successful architect brother. She'd taken enough "handouts" from Ed without considering the consequences. No, she needed to succeed on her own merits, as much as possible, as long as Eddie's health or happiness wasn't compromised. Living rent-free over Travis's garage in a nice but small apartment helped tremendously, even though the few pieces of heirloom furniture she'd managed to keep after the estate sale seemed lonely and sad against the stark white walls and light wood flooring.

"It's just that I've always thought of myself as a homemaker and a mother, not a sole provider," she explained to Jodie. "Although I know how important it is to be independent, sometimes I feel that I can't do this alone."

"Yes, you can." Jodie gave Kate a fierce hug. "Besides, you're not alone. You have us, for better or for worse. And everyone in town loves you."

Kate nodded even as she thought of one person who wasn't so fond of her inquisitive son—their neighbor Luke Simon. Still, she hugged Jodie back and felt better now that she'd expressed her fears. She wasn't a wimp. She *would* get a job and she *would* be strong for Eddie.

"Okay, I'll leave you alone with the laundry. I just came down to tell you that we're going into town. Travis needs to stop by the hardware store, then we're joining Hank and Gwendolyn for an early dinner at Bretford House. We'd love for you and Eddie to join us."

"I'm not sure. He's still napping after his little visit to the pasture." Talking about Eddie brought Kate's thoughts back to their neighbor. Luke could be at the hardware store, or just around town…or with Hank and Gwendolyn for dinner out. Ever since that first nonmeeting at the café, Kate had been unexpectedly conscious of him. She could barely talk to him, even to apologize for her son's transgressions. The man flustered her more than she'd been flustered in a long, long time.

"Oh? Did he cross the fence again?"

Kate held up the shirt. "There's evidence he did, though I didn't get a call." Kate sighed. "I don't know why Eddie's so interested in those animals."

"Oh, come on, Kate. Zebras in the Texas Hill Country? A floppy-eared donkey and two matching white horses? Of course he's curious. I just wish he'd listen to our warnings. Like you said, he walks—or runs, probably—across our pasture with those longhorns out there. They seem gentle, but those horns are deadly."

"I know. He loves being outdoors. I had to be so protective when we lived on a busy street in the suburbs. I'd hate to confine him to the apartment here."

"No, you can't do that. Children need time to play. It's too bad he's such a sneaky escape artist—and I mean that in the nicest way."

Kate laughed as she stuffed the shirt into the washer. "I know exactly what you mean. Wait until Marsha starts crawling and walking. You'll get a real workout then."

"Speaking of workouts, I'd better change. Bretford House isn't formal, but I don't like to go there dressed like I should be in yoga class or going for a jog."

Kate looked down at her own jeans and sweatshirt. "I'd have to change, too, and I still have a lot of work to do. Maybe I'll pass tonight. You and Travis have a double date with Gwendolyn and Hank."

"And our two little monsters? I'm sure they're bringing their little boy, so dinner should be interesting with both kids teething. Come to think of it, maybe you *should* stay home!"

Kate chuckled, then Jodie said, "Well, I'm going to get dressed. If you change your mind, be ready in about a half an hour. Otherwise, we'll see you tomorrow for church."

"Yes, that's the plan. If Eddie doesn't run off again."

"Good luck," Jodie said with a smile, then turned and walked out of the garage.

Good luck. Kate knew she'd need it to avoid Luke Simon for the rest of her stay in Ranger Springs. Or, if she got a teaching job here, for the rest of her life. She didn't want that flustered feeling, she especially didn't want to get involved with a man, and she extra-especially didn't want to encourage Eddie's interest in what should clearly be off-limits—exotic animals and a Harley-riding Californian.

With a sigh, Kate added detergent and started the wash cycle.

THE FOLLOWING Saturday morning after breakfast, Eddie excused himself to play soldier in the backyard. Kate didn't approve of the game, but Travis had played it with him after Eddie had seen coverage of the war on television. They both claimed that Kate, being a "girl," just didn't understand "guy things."

Kate settled into her couch with her second cup of coffee and listened to Eddie's new toy gun's *ratta-tat-tat* as he ran from tree to tree. He should have a playmate. She hoped he made friends at the elementary school. Perhaps when she got a permanent job, she'd rent a house in town where there were other children his age. She didn't want her son growing up lonely.

Pushing aside her misgivings about Eddie playing soldier, she picked up a professional teachers organization's magazine and turned to an article she'd tagged. During her years of marriage, she hadn't kept up with educational standards and was sadly behind in understanding funding issues, certification requirements and classroom trends. Before long she was immersed in her reading. When she turned the page, she heard…silence.

The *ratta-tat-tat* had stopped. There was no sound of her son scurrying from tree to tree. Nothing but the chirping of birds.

She hurried out the door onto the small landing at the top of the stairs and called, "Eddie!"

Nothing.

She ran down the steps, calling him again. And again. No Eddie.

Travis stepped outside onto his deck, baby Marsha in his arms. "What's wrong?"

"I think Eddie has run off again."

"If you wait, I'll take you in the pickup." Travis kept an old truck for driving across his rolling pastures to feed his longhorns, especially in the winters.

"No, he was just outside playing. I think I can catch up with him. Then I'm grounding him until he's thirty."

Travis unclipped his cell phone from his waistband. "Take this in case you need to call."

"Thanks. I keep forgetting mine."

"You should always have a cell phone with you, Kate. Or a walkie-talkie. I'll get some for us. Be careful."

"It's just a pasture."

"I know."

She rushed off, grateful she was wearing a comfortable pair of jeans, a turtleneck and sneakers, her "suburban mom" uniform. At the edge of the backyard she discovered Eddie's empty juice box. Following the path two little feet had worked into the winter-dry grass wasn't difficult. Eddie had obviously walked this way many times. Too many times, she silently corrected herself.

By the time she arrived at the wire fence separating Travis's property from Luke Simon's ranch, she was out of breath. "I've got to start exercising again," she whispered as she placed her hands on her knees and breathed deeply. Keeping up with one six-year-old was difficult enough, but soon she'd be charged with handling about twenty energetic elementary students on a daily basis. If she got the job.

To her left she heard the faint sound of her son singing his favorite song. Relief swept through her, because although she didn't doubt that he'd once again migrated to see the odd animals—and their equally mysterious owner—she was now sure he was safe.

She'd just glimpsed his red shirt when the roar of a powerful engine disturbed the nature sounds. Looking toward Luke Simon's driveway, she saw a large silver crew-cab pickup move toward the run-down ranch house.

Curious, knowing she shouldn't be, she jogged to the row of trees dividing the pasture and the driveway.

"Luke!" a female voice called from the truck as the engine died. "Where are you?"

A door banged shut. A few seconds later, Luke appeared, dressed in tight, faded jeans and a white T-shirt. His long hair was disheveled and his feet bare.

Kate sucked in a breath. He looked like a movie star. A Greek god. *Stop staring at him,* she told herself. *Concentrate on your son.*

Eddie was crouched behind a large oak, also watching the group that had arrived in the noisy pickup, and seemingly unaware that his mother had followed him.

"What the hell are you guys doing here?"

Luke's clearly disbelieving tone carried through the trees. Just then, a big-busted blonde bounced from the truck, giggling as she jogged toward him. *It's a wonder she doesn't seriously hurt herself,* Kate thought, glancing down at her own modest B-cups.

"Luke! We missed you so much that we had to visit."

"I can't believe you moved to the middle of nowhere!" an equally well-endowed redhead squealed, also running over to him. Both women hugged him, one on each side, until Kate thought he might be crushed by silicone. Or whatever doctors were implanting now.

It was *Baywatch on the Prairie.*

"You don't like my ranch?" Luke asked.

"It's so…rural!" the blonde exclaimed.

A California-style cowboy eased around the front of the truck and grinned. Dressed in new jeans and a flashy snap-front shirt, he "wasn't from around here," as they said in town. "I couldn't keep them away," he said.

"I just hadn't expected to see you guys in Texas."

"We're working on a movie just outside of Austin. We've got today and tomorrow off while they add new sets, so here we are," the man said.

"I'm not exactly set up for guests," Luke replied.

The blonde hugged him so tight she nearly knocked him off balance. Kate almost snorted at the ridiculous display. But then, Luke was probably used to that kind of attention from that type of woman.

"That's okay, honey. We can sleep anywhere."

The redhead giggled. The California cowboy laughed and slapped Luke on the back, and then headed toward the house.

Eddie chose that moment to dart from his hiding place, across the driveway toward the small pasture where the two zebras, their long fuzzy ears twitching, sized up the newcomers.

Luke and the others turned at the sound of Eddie's tennis shoes crunching the gravel. Kate cringed, knowing she'd have to reveal herself, hoping they didn't assume she'd been lurking in the bushes, watching the tawdry scene. Which of course was exactly what she'd been doing.

She made a lot of noise rustling bushes, then called out, "Eddie! You come back here right now!"

All eyes were on her as she stumbled out of the tree line, got her balance and dashed across the drive. She hated doing this. Making a scene in front of Luke Simon's guests. His gorgeous, movie-people guests.

"Sorry for the interruption," Kate said, breathless. "I'll just get Eddie and we'll be gone."

"Well, aren't you cute?" The blonde peeled herself off Luke and turned to Eddie, perhaps fifteen feet away near the fence, frozen because he knew he'd been discovered. The little scamp.

Kate rushed over, putting her arm around him before the blonde could crush him to her unnaturally large chest. No telling what trauma would be revealed when he was an adult!

The group followed the blonde until they were all standing there, staring at Kate and Eddie as though they were oddities.

"These animals can be dangerous," Luke said to Eddie in a surprisingly patient and focused voice. "I told you before that you can't come over here by yourself."

"He's not by himself," Kate said. "I'm with him now, and I'm taking him home, and he's not going to bother you again, are you, Eddie?"

"No, ma'am."

"Oh, isn't that cute?" the blonde gushed again, reaching for Eddie. "He's so polite."

Kate pulled him behind her. "Excuse me. We'll be going now."

"Well, sheesh, lady, we're not going to contaminate him," the redhead said.

Luke frowned, but Kate didn't wait for the scene to get any uglier. She grasped Eddie's hand and said, "Apologize to Mr. Simon."

"I'm sorry I tried to see the zebras again."

Luke nodded.

"And I'm sorry we interrupted your…party," Kate added. She tugged her son across the drive, toward the cover of the trees and the safety of her brother's ranch.

LATE THAT AFTERNOON, Luke excused himself from his unexpected—and frankly, unwanted—guests to take care of a little business. Or so he told them. He needed to get away for a few minutes. Their arrival, combined with Eddie's surprise visit and Kate's even more surprising arrival, had left him shaken. And Kate's snobby reaction to his friends—more like former coworkers—had clearly defined their differences. She didn't even want Marlena to touch her son.

Kate would be shocked if she knew how often Luke had thought about touching *her*. Not that he had any right to think about the woman. It was apparent she was one of those women who never associated with a working guy, and her behavior today had driven that point home. Her brother was rich, and she'd obviously grown up dripping in money. She wore classic clothes and drove a sensible car and had a polite son who just wanted to be a kid.

Well, the hell with her. If she was too good for them, she could just stay on her side of the fence.

Paul, Shelby and Marlena were high-energy, high-maintenance people. When he'd worked on a movie set with them, they'd been tolerable, even fun. Here in the quiet of the ranch, they seemed as out of place as a…well, a zebra in Texas.

As he walked back from the mailbox at the end of his driveway, he speculated that maybe they'd want to go out later. He'd been to Shultze's Roadhouse several times for a beer and a burger and found the place entertaining. The jukebox played country and western, and Texas-oriented beer signs hung on the walls. Marlena and Shelby would gush at the "authentic" decor. As soon as he sorted the mail, he'd recommend they visit the local hangout. Without him.

Several bills, a handful of catalogs—nothing unusual. Then a carefully hand-printed address caught his attention. He didn't know anyone in Florida.

He slit the envelope and pulled out a letter. A photo—the kind taken by school photographers—fell to the desk. He picked it up and looked at the little girl's face. A sense of déjà vu rushed over him, as though he'd seen her before. But he knew he hadn't, so after studying her sun-streaked dark brown hair and amazingly mature brown eyes, he leaned the photo against the lamp and began to read.

"Dear Mr. Simon," the letter began, neatly printed like the envelope. "You don't know me, but nearly nine years ago you knew my sister, Shawna Jacobs."

Luke's heart skipped a beat as he remembered his late mother's former coworker. Shawna had been a pretty, helpful and sympathetic friend when he'd needed one, lending a hand as he sorted through his mother's belongings after her untimely death. Comfort had turned to passion, and for a week or so he'd shared Shawna's bed.

He'd been young, the sex fumbling but energetic. She'd claimed she was on the pill. He hadn't given the consequences a second thought.

He looked back at the photo. No. It couldn't be....

Chapter Two

Luke continued reading with a mixture of excitement and dread. "My sister tried to contact you after you went away, but she couldn't find you in California because she thought your name was Moretti, the same as your mother's. I just found out your real last name and tracked you down on the Internet."

Luke's mother, Angela Moretti, had never married. His father, Ronald Lucas Simon, already had a family when he seduced and deserted her. The bastard.

"This will come as a big surprise, but you have a daughter. Brittany is eight years old and in the third grade. Right now, she needs you because Shawna is dead and I'm driving long haul starting in a month."

No! his mind screamed. Shawna might have been on the pill, but no birth control was one hundred percent foolproof. She could have had his baby. It was possible.

He wished Shawna were alive to ask. He wished he'd thought of her after driving away from his mother's apartment nearly nine years ago. He was sorry Shawna was dead, but the truth was, she hadn't meant much to him. He felt especially bad about that now, considering she'd had a child. Maybe his child, he thought, shaking his head.

He knew nothing about children, except that they were frequently loud and often unruly. Just look at Eddie Wooten, who kept disobeying his mother and coming across the fence. Luke had no idea how to stop that child from indulging his fascination with the ponies and zebras. How in the world could he relate to an eight-year-old girl?

Plus, this ranch was barely livable, except for the animals. Their barn was repaired, their fences secure. They had plenty of food and fresh water. But a human, a little girl? He didn't know how to feed a child, much less bathe and dress one for school.

He may be a father, but he was nowhere near being a dad.

Luke pushed away his panic and continued reading. "You'll need to get all this approved by a judge. I've already contacted the court here in Florida, since my parents are both dead and I don't have any other relatives. I guess you'll also want to meet Brittany. I'm hoping you can come to Florida right away." Shawna's brother, Andy Jacobs, gave his home and cell phone numbers and asked Luke to call him as soon as he got the letter. He closed by asking Luke not to waste time; the long-haul trucking job he'd taken started in a month and Brittany had nowhere else to go.

If Luke didn't claim his daughter, she'd become a ward of the state. A foster child. Unwanted. Deserted by the only two people who had cared for her.

He wouldn't let that happen. Not if she were really his child.

Clutching the letter, Luke sat down on a desk chair that creaked in protest. Of all the things that could have happened to him, of all the twists and turns of his life, this was the most incredible.

He'd never thought about having children. And if he ever did decide to, he certainly would have expected them far, far into the future. Not this month, on a ranch that was barely functional. Not a *girl*, for pity's sake, and one already eight years old.

He didn't know what to do. Except that he would go to Florida to see her, and if she was indeed his daughter, he would claim her as his own.

Paul, Shelby and Marlena burst through the door, laughing and chatting, bringing Luke back to the present. He placed the letter, printed side down, on the desk.

"Say, we're getting hungry. Is there a place to go out around here? Beer's on me," Paul said.

"Shultze's Roadhouse is on the state highway, just a couple of miles from here," Luke replied, still seated. He glanced again at Brittany's photo, leaning against the lamp. She resembled him, he realized. That's why she'd seemed so familiar. She had his coloring and his eyes. Her mouth and wavy hair were Shawna's.

"Hey, who's that?" Shelby asked.

"She's...that's Brittany."

"Cute kid. A relative?"

Luke looked up at his friends. They were completely out of place here in Ranger Springs, just as he was completely out of place as a father. But still, that's what he was—most probably—and he'd darn well better get used to it.

"She's my daughter," he said simply.

"Oh. Oh, wow." Marlena appeared almost as stunned as he felt. "I didn't know you had a kid."

"A daughter. She's eight." He picked up the photo and stared at Brittany's image again, a slow smile forming. "I didn't know either, until today." He got up from the chair and turned to Paul. "You guys go on without me. I have to get my ranch ready for a little girl."

"You sure?" Paul asked. "We could have a good time."

"I'm sure. It's been good seeing you again, but things have changed." He looked down at Brittany's photo again, thinking about his ranch, his responsibilities, and his vow to live a quiet, low-key life. "Everything has changed."

AS SHE STOOD on her small balcony watching the sun set over the trees between her brother's property and Luke Simon's ranch, Kate mentally kicked herself for her earlier behavior. She'd come across as an incompetent mother for not keeping Eddie at home, not to mention a klutz as she stumbled out of the tree line and into Luke's little party. They might even think she was a snoop, since she had been listening and watching a private rendezvous. To top it off, she'd offended the grasping *Baywatch*-like blonde who had almost gotten her hands on Eddie. Kate couldn't believe that when she'd faced Luke Simon up close, her brain had just stopped working, unable to communicate anything intelligent to her mouth. How she had to have seemed to him and his visitors!

Okay, so Luke Simon's friends' opinions of her shouldn't matter all that much. But she really didn't want to offend him, especially because Eddie consistently violated the neighborly boundaries. Having a child continually ignore his warnings, plus having that child's mother invade his privacy, wasn't any way to welcome a newcomer to town.

Not that she should be a one-woman welcoming committee. She certainly wasn't on par with the other women in his life. The blonde and the redhead were stunning. They might not be natural beauties, but they were gorgeous nonetheless. He probably knew plenty of Hollywood actors and actresses, and they were far removed from regular people in a small town—except her sister-in-law, Jodie, of course, who was both famous and beautiful.

But Kate knew she was an ordinary-looking divorced mother, one who was barely coping on her own. The last thing—the very last thing—she should do was dwell on her unwilling fascination with their bad-boy neighbor.

Okay, maybe now he appeared more like a cowboy than a biker, but he projected a devil-may-care persona that was completely foreign to her. She'd never known anyone like Luke Simon. She'd never dated anyone remotely as daring and attractive as him. She'd always gone for proper and dependable—and look how well that had turned out!—so why did she think of him so often?

Probably because she was at the point in her life where she'd been forced to change. If Ed hadn't misused his clients' money and had an affair, she would have continued with the marriage, at least for Eddie's sake. Her marriage to Ed hadn't been even close to exciting in the last few years, but she'd grown accustomed to the blandness and the comfort. Now she was suddenly single and broke, over thirty and starting a new life, and why wouldn't she be attracted to Luke Simon? He was, like a movie star or fictional character, compelling from afar. She had no intention of getting any closer than the boundary of his fence.

With a sigh, Kate pushed away from the railing at the top of the stairs. The sun was setting, the day almost over, and she had to talk to Eddie about his behavior. She had to make him understand that fences were important barriers—for children *and* their mothers!

AFTER PAUL, SHELBY and Marlena left the ranch for Shultze's Roadhouse and to hopefully find a place to stay for the night, Luke got on the phone to check for flights into the Orlando area. Brittany lived in a small town nearby the theme-oriented center of Florida. He wondered if she liked Mickey and the gang, or if she cared more for the new characters he saw on television. Or if she liked video games or stuffed animals more, if she went to movies or would rather play outside.

Maybe there were things kids did that he couldn't even imagine. He knew nothing of those new MP3 players, for example, and could barely operate a computer. There wasn't much of a need for high-tech skills in animal training and stunt work. He happily left that stuff to the business types who invested in horses or breeding stock and the movie special-effects folks.

He picked up the phone and dialed his friend Hank, whose land adjoined Travis Whitaker's to the west. Luke breathed a sigh of relief when Hank answered after the second ring.

"Hank, it's Luke."

"What's up? You getting your zoo all settled in?"

"Yeah, the animals are doing great. Something else has come up, though, and I need your help."

"Sure, buddy. What can I do for you?"

"I'm going to need some repairs and changes made to the house over here, and I'm going to need them fast. I don't have any idea who to call."

"What's the rush?"

Luke ran a hand around his aching neck. The tension was getting to him. "I just got some news that changed my plans." He paused, taking a deep breath. "Apparently I have an eight-year-old daughter."

"Wow. How did that happen?"

Luke chuckled. "The usual way. One man, one woman, faulty birth control." He'd believed Shawna was on the pill when he'd revealed he had no protection. Now he wasn't sure what to think.

"Yeah, but why didn't you know until now?"

"Shawna was a friend of my mother. She assumed my last name was the same as my mother's—Moretti—and telling her any different would have required an explanation of the worthless piece of—well, just say the man my mother thought she was madly in love with. So I kept quiet and figured I never would see or hear from Shawna again. And I didn't." Luke sighed. "I got a letter from her brother today, then I talked to him on the phone. Shawna died in a car accident recently and he's been taking care of her daughter. Er, my daughter. He's going to start a new job and can't look after her any longer."

"Wow, that's some story. You must have been shocked."

"Believe me, I was. I haven't thought about Shawna, to tell you the truth. We only spent about a week together right after my mother died. She helped me sort through my mother's things and we got close. Her brother said she tried to contact me, which I believe. Shawna was a nice woman." He felt bad that she'd died, especially never getting to tell him the news that she'd gotten pregnant.

"So, are you sure the girl is yours?"

"Pretty sure. She looks a lot like me."

"Still, it might be a good idea to get some tests done."

"I will, once I go to Florida. I'll check with her family doctor. I'm sure we can get it done there."

"Okay. Good thinking." Luke heard Hank sigh. "So now you're going to raise your daughter, if she's really yours?"

"Yes, I am." Every time Luke looked at the photo, he became more convinced that Brittany was his child. "That's why I need the house fixed up. I've repaired the barn and fences, but not the main house. It's in pretty sad shape."

"Yeah, it is, which is why you got it cheap."

"Right. Personally, I've stayed in worse places, and at least the plumbing and electrical work, but I have to get it up to 'little girl' standards since I'll have to be approved by the court to get custody of Brittany. And everything has to be done in a month."

"I see what you mean. Well, I can recommend Nate Branson, Jimmy Mack's brother. He just moved back to town due to all the construction in the area. Gina Mae Summers, the Realtor, told me he does good work."

"I'm having trouble keeping up with all these folks. Jimmy Mack is…?"

"Jimmy Mack Branson. The hardware store owner. We met him when you bought the supplies for the tack room."

"Oh, right." Hank had taken him around the town and introduced him to a dozen people, but the ones he remembered most clearly were Kate Wooten and her son, hovered over by her brother Travis Whitaker. "Should I call Jimmy Mack to get in touch with his brother?"

"Why don't you call Gina? Her office number is listed, and you won't be bothering her if you call late either, because she's single."

"Single? Are you matchmaking? Because I've got to tell you, the last thing on my mind right now is women." Well, any woman except Kate, who kept creeping into his thoughts despite her obvious caution—maybe even dislike—of him and his friends. "I'm not about to mess up my relationship with my daughter by dating any woman."

"Okay, I'm just trying to help."

"I'm going to book a flight to Florida so I can meet Brittany and get those tests done. Can I get you to check my place? I hired Carlos to help out, but some of the animals need medicine daily."

"Sure, leave me a list and I'll take care of things."

"Thanks, Hank. It's good to have a friend here."

"You'd have lots of friends if you'd let the folks around here get to know you."

If he was open and honest, people would soon realize his father was a multimillionaire who'd died and left most of his money to his legitimate family, but quite a healthy bequest to his bastard son, whom he'd never acknowledged in life. And once that fact was public, the persistent biographer, who was doing a tell-all book about Ronald Lucas Simon, would be in Ranger Springs faster than Luke could say "hell, no."

No, the best thing was to keep to himself. "Yeah,

well, if they're 'friendly' like my neighbor Travis Whitaker, I wouldn't depend on them to 'help' me out at all."

"Travis just got the wrong idea about you when you first got into town," Hank said.

"Why? I'm not after his property or his wife."

"No, but she and his sister expressed some…curiosity when you pulled up to the café on your Harley."

"Oh, that." He'd enjoyed the road trip from California to Texas, taking his time to see the deserts and small towns along the way, thinking about how his life was about to change. Little did he know that he'd be getting more than a variety of aging animals and 640 acres of land. "I still don't understand what I've done to make him testy."

"He's just protective. His sister Kate went through a messy divorce, and she's having a hard time making ends meet, from what I've heard."

"You're kidding! She looks like she's always had money, always will."

"Travis and Kate's mother was an actress and their father was wealthy—oil money out in West Texas. They didn't do without much as kids, except maybe some stability at home, if you know what I mean."

Luke thought back to how he and his mother had struggled to pay the bills each month. They didn't have much, but he knew he could always depend on her, so in a way, he'd had stability. What he didn't have was a father—not that he'd really needed one. His mother, however, had loved Ronald Lucas Simon even though the SOB had never paid a dime of child support or expressed any interest in his illegitimate son. At least, not until recently. "Yeah, I know what you mean."

"Well, I'll let you go and make those phone calls. Give me a buzz when you've made your plans."

Luke ended the call and sat back in his desk chair. So, Kate wasn't currently wealthy and her divorce had been messy. And she was curious about him. At least, according to Hank. Kate sure didn't *show* it. Every time he'd seen her, she'd seemed perturbed by him, as if she'd like to turn up her nose and stalk away, but her manners were good to make such a scene.

Big deal. Luke didn't need friendly neighbors, and he certainly didn't want to get tied up with a woman right now. Soon he'd have his daughter. They'd be just fine together, just as he and his mother had been just fine.

But first, he needed to do two things: get in touch with Brittany's uncle about the travel plans *and* make arrangements to fix up this house. He didn't want to give the authorities any reason to keep him from being a father, especially when he wasn't sure what court approval would involve.

He'd never abandon his child as Ronald Simon had deserted him.

With new resolve, he dialed Andy Jacobs in Florida, half hoping that Brittany would answer the phone so he could hear her voice for the first time, half dreading talking to her when he didn't know what to say.

The phone was answered on the third ring and Luke sighed in relief. "Hello, Mr. Jacobs. This is Luke Simon." He took another deep breath. "I'm coming to Florida to see Brittany."

Chapter Three

Kate had a substitute teaching assignment at the Ranger Springs Elementary School two days later. She was glad for the experience and the money substituting provided, but the assignments threw her off balance because they usually called her around six o'clock in the morning. She always had to make sure her schedule coincided with Eddie's, just in case she was teaching at the middle school or high school.

Today, her feet hurt from chasing twenty second-graders around the classroom and playground and all she wanted to do was soak in the big bathtub for about an hour. Instead, she knew she'd have her hands full with Eddie because his class had taken a field trip to Cheryl Jacks's petting zoo. He'd chatted nonstop since they'd gotten in the car to drive home. He loved animals so much. He wanted a dog, a cat, a hamster…or a zebra.

"Bring your lunch bag and come on inside," she told him as she parked the car.

"I want to go outside to play."

"I know, and you can, but let me get settled in first. Since I taught today, I need to change clothes. And I bet you'd like some string cheese and apple slices."

"Ooookay," he replied, reluctant resignation temporarily replacing his childish excitement. He dragged his already scuffed sneakers across the carpet as Kate headed for the kitchen.

She fixed his snack and he asked if he could eat it outside, because maybe Aunt Jodie would bring baby Marsha out. Kate agreed, thankful for a little time to herself to freshen up. Still, she watched him to make sure he headed for their deck, not Luke Simon's property.

She prayed the talk she'd had with Eddie after his last transgression had finally sunk in. Besides the danger involved in running off, she'd been acutely embarrassed when she'd popped out of the trees and surprised Luke and his guests. She didn't want to be in that situation again.

In her bathroom, she stripped off her schoolteacher clothes and threw them into the hamper. She had a smear of tempura paint on her denim skirt and a spot of ketchup on her flower-embroidered pullover. Hopefully, both stains would come out in the wash, but at the moment, she couldn't work up much energy for prespotting.

Just as she pulled on an old pair of gym shorts and a baggy T-shirt, the phone rang. She wanted to check on Eddie, but after seeing the caller ID, she knew she needed to answer the phone first.

Five minutes later, she felt on top of the world. The school administrators wanted to make sure her application was on file with the district for a teaching job.

As she hung up the phone, her smile was as big as her hopes for a permanent position. Although she hadn't taught full-time since she was a student teacher eight years ago, she now saw there was a chance to provide a home for Eddie and herself. She could move out of Travis's garage apartment and rent a house of her own.

One with a safe yard for Eddie to play in.

Eddie! He was on the deck alone. What if Jodie hadn't come outside with the baby?

Kate flung open the door and jogged down the steps. She was probably overreacting, but he'd proved that he could be very sneaky about leaving the yard.

Sure enough, there was Jodie with Marsha in her arms. "Where's Eddie?" she asked.

Kate stopped, her smile fading. "I was just about to ask you."

Jodie propped her six-month-old on her left hip. "We just stepped outside, and I haven't seen Eddie."

Oh no! Not again. Kate took off at a run toward Luke Simon's property.

LUKE WAS on the phone, finalizing his hotel plans in Orlando, when he heard the commotion. The donkey began to bray, and he heard the thundering of small hooves in the nearby pasture. By the time he had come out of his chair and rushed to the door, the frightened squeal of a child cut through the afternoon.

When Luke got to the fence, both zebras were awkwardly running toward the trees, where the ponies and the donkey stood trembling, their ears raised, ready to flee. At first he couldn't tell what had frightened them so. He scanned the pasture, expecting to see Eddie Wooten running at them with his arms flapping.

Instead, he saw a limp heap of blue and white lying maybe three feet from the fence, by the row of trees.

The pile of clothes moved, one small sneaker pushing against the ground.

"Oh, no," he muttered as he vaulted the fence and raced across the pasture. His heart beat hard from more than the mad dash. He'd told Eddie several times to stay away, to quit trying to get close to the zebras. They were tame, and although they'd been raised around people, they weren't domesticated animals. When frightened, there was no telling what they'd do. Their natural instincts were far stronger than those of horses, mules or donkeys.

As he neared the little boy, he heard Kate calling, "Eddie!"

"He's over here," Luke called out, sliding to a stop in the slippery new grass. "Here, by the mesquite trees."

Eddie whimpered, his arms and legs moving. *Thank God.*

"The what?" she yelled. "Where are you?"

Luke stood up and waved. "Over here!"

Kate ran toward them as Luke went down on one knee.

"Eddie, I need you to tell me where it hurts. Come on, buddy, stop crying."

Eddie looked up at him, still whimpering, but the little boy reached up and rubbed his eyes. *That's a good sign,* Luke told himself. "Can you wiggle your feet?"

Sniffling, Eddie looked down at his stained athletic shoes and moved both feet back and forth.

"Good boy."

"Eddie!" Kate dropped to the ground and reached for her son.

Luke put a hand on her shoulder. "Wait! I was just making sure he hasn't injured his back."

"His back? Oh, my God. I wasn't thinking.... Eddie, are you okay?"

"I don't know, Mommy. My leg hurts and my hand hurts." He held up his scratched right hand, traces of grass and blood making his mother gasp.

Luke turned to look at Kate. "Are *you* all right? I think Eddie's going to be fine, but let's be calm, okay?"

"Calm. Yes, I can be calm," she replied, taking a deep breath. "Thank you."

That threw him a curve. The very last thing he'd expected was a *thank-you* from the mother of the little boy lying in his pasture.

"Eddie, does your back hurt?"

"Not too much. Not like my hand."

"Okay, that's good. How about your head?" Luke held up two fingers. "How many fingers do you see?"

"Two," Eddie replied, holding up two of his own on his left hand.

"Good boy," Luke said, smiling.

"That's right," Kate said, forcing a smile. "I'm going to check your leg, sweetie. Hold real still."

She was very calm now, very motherly as she inspected his limbs. Apparently, Eddie had fallen on the side of his hip, not really his leg, and it was probably bruised.

"I don't think you broke anything, but let's get you to the doctor," Luke said.

"I should call an ambulance," Kate said.

"Travis told me there isn't an ambulance in Ranger Springs, and I don't think this is serious enough for a CareFlight helicopter, do you?"

"Well, probably not." She looked around as though she was getting her bearings. "I need to take him to the medical clinic."

"I'll call ahead."

"I should have brought my cell phone," Kate said. "Travis is always getting after me to carry it, but I usually forget. When Eddie runs off, I just go after him."

Luke didn't want to say anything about her brother, her errant son or her impulsive behavior, so he kept quiet. She had enough to deal with right now.

"Mommy, I want to go home."

"I need to make sure you're okay, sweetie. We're going to see Dr. Amy."

"I don't want to see the doctor! She'll give me a shot."

"Come on, buddy," Luke said, scooping the boy up in his arms and rising. "I'll bet the doctor is real nice."

"I wanna go home!" Eddie tried to wiggle out of Luke's grasp, but he held firm. He wasn't about to let a six-year-old get the best of him, especially in front of Kate.

"Eddie, be still! You could be hurt," she said, leaning close. Close enough for Luke to feel her warmth and smell her fragrance of flowers and fear. He wanted to reach out and envelop her along with her son, to tell her everything would be okay. But that wasn't his responsibility any more than commenting on her personal life was, so he simply headed to his truck.

"You're going to take Eddie and me to the clinic?" Kate asked, walking quickly to match his longer stride.

He glanced down at her. "Seems like a good idea."

"You don't have to. If you'll just take me home—"

"No, I'm taking you to the clinic." They reached the fence and he paused. "Go on over and I'll hand Eddie to you."

Kate slipped through the rails, apparently unconcerned about how her loose shorts revealed her upper thighs, or how the soft knit fabric of her shirt caressed her curves. Luke knew he shouldn't be thinking such thoughts as he held her injured son, but he couldn't help admiring the mother. Quickly, he handed Eddie across the fence, being careful not to brush his fingers against her breasts as he released the little boy.

"I have to get my keys," he said, stepping between the rails. "Walk toward the truck. I'll be right there."

He jogged to the house—not an easy feat in boots—and returned with his wallet and keys. Kate was already seated inside the truck, holding Eddie on her lap.

"Seat belt?" Luke asked.

"Oh, right." She placed the boy on the bench seat between them and hooked him in. "Are you okay, sweetie? You aren't hurting too much, are you?"

"I wanna go home. I'm sorry I fell off the zebra."

"You tried to ride a zebra!" Kate exclaimed. "Eddie, no!"

"I'm sorry, Mommy," he said softly, about to cry.

"Hey, we can talk about that later, okay?" Kate obviously loved Eddie very much and was at a loss to stop his wandering and inquisitive nature. Being a parent was tough, something he was about to experience firsthand...if he could get his house and his life in order in just twenty-seven days.

Kate hugged Eddie to her and appeared close to tears herself when Luke glanced at her. Then he was on the curving road leading over the hills toward town, and he didn't look at mother and son again.

KATE BREATHED a sigh of relief when Dr. Amy Wheatley Phillips pronounced Eddie bruised but not broken. No nerve damage, just a contusion on his hip and another on his hand, which he'd scraped raw during his fall.

"You must take it easy for at least a week," the doctor told Eddie. "No falling around or getting any more injuries, okay?" She looked at Kate and winked. "And you need long, warm baths, Eddie. At least one a day. That will make the bruise go away faster."

"Baths! Yuck. Do I have to?"

Dr. Amy smiled and stroked Eddie's mussed hair. "Absolutely, young man. Your mother knows best, so you mind her and you'll get well very soon."

Eddie frowned and swung his legs over the edge of the exam table, appearing even younger and more forlorn than Kate ever remembered. The cotton gown wrapped around him like a big, soft tablecloth. Or maybe a receiving blanket, as if he were a baby again.

Oh, those were the days, when she could keep him safe. Protect him from the dangers of life.

"Come back and see me if you have any problems."

"Thank you, Dr. Amy," Kate said.

"You're welcome. And Eddie? Don't ever try to ride anyone else's animals. In Texas, back in the old days, that could be considered rustling. Only the bad guys tried to steal someone else's animals."

"I didn't try to steal the zebra!"

"Using anything that doesn't belong to you is stealing, Eddie," Kate explained. "Using the zebra for a ride is something that Mr. Simon didn't want you to do, and that means you tried to steal a ride."

Eddie folded his arms across his chest and frowned.

"We'll talk about this at home, young man, after you apologize to Mr. Simon."

"Gladys told me he brought the two of you in," Dr. Amy said as she removed her rubber gloves and dropped them into the biohazard trash.

"Yes, I'm afraid I was a bit of a basket case. Your receptionist was wonderful, by the way. Very calm in the face of my near-hysteria."

"I'm sure it's very difficult to see your own child lying injured in a pasture."

"Exactly," Kate said, frowning at her adventurous son.

"I'm glad Mr. Simon was there for you, then. I'm sure he was more objective."

"Yes, he was…great." Kate wasn't happy to realize how true her words were. Part of her wanted to be angry at him for having the tempting animals. Part of her wanted to resent him for his appeal, both to her and to Eddie. But he had been sensible when she felt the urge to rant and cry and hold Eddie tight. He'd been…great.

"See Gladys on your way out," Dr. Amy said as she left the examination room.

Within minutes, Eddie was dressed in his stained, rumpled clothes and Kate had given Gladys the insurance information. Only then did Kate look to the waiting room to see if Luke Simon was still there.

Or if he'd taken off because he didn't want to spend any more time than necessary with a hysterical woman and a meddlesome child.

She inhaled deeply when she saw him, one arm stretched along the back of a couch, booted foot crossed and resting on his knee. His long, dark hair was ruffled as if by the wind or his own fingers plowing through the thick strands. He looked far too good for her peace of mind, just as tempting and exciting as when he'd strolled into the Four Square Café several months ago.

He appeared relaxed at first, but she noticed a bit of tension in his expression, as though he had a lot on his mind. He probably had a ton of chores to do at his ranch. He'd dashed off and left everything. Had he been alone, or were those Hollywood people still there?

She wasn't going to think about those gorgeous women anymore. Comparing herself to others that physically perfect was an exercise in futility, especially when she was dressed in old shorts and a faded T-shirt.

"We're ready," she said just loud enough to get his attention, "if you're willing to drive us home."

"How's Eddie?" Luke asked, rising effortlessly from the couch. Kate nearly sighed when she thought about how strong he had to be to move so gracefully.

"He's going to be fine, if he's careful and takes lots of warm baths."

"Yuck!"

Kate leaned down to eye level with her son. "Eddie, don't you have something to say to Mr. Simon?"

Eddie nodded. "I'm sorry I tried to ride the zebra, Mr. Simon," he said in a small voice. "I didn't mean to steal anything."

Luke appeared confused, glancing at her for clarification.

Kate hid her smile by biting her lips. "Dr. Amy told him about how taking something, even a ride on someone's animal, is like stealing."

"You didn't steal from me," Luke said. "I'm really concerned about the zebra, though."

"Why?" Eddie asked.

Luke hunkered down in front of Eddie. "Because she's pretty old and she has arthritis."

"Just like Grandpa Whitaker," Kate explained.

"His fingers are all knobby," Eddie said.

"Well, her knees are kind of like that and it hurts her to move. She likes to graze real slow beside her friend. When she has to move fast, like to run away from something that scares her, her knees hurt."

Eddie looked as though he was about to cry. "I didn't mean to hurt her. I thought she'd like to go for a ride."

"Riding is a lot more fun for the person riding than for the animal being ridden," Luke explained. "Besides, zebras are wild animals. They want to buck whenever they feel weight on their back. That's why people don't ride them in Africa, where they're from. Over there, the wild zebras buck off the lions and other predators who try to eat them."

"Wow. I didn't know that," Eddie said.

Listening to Luke Simon was a lot like watching a very sexy host on the Discovery Channel. Except none of the hosts were as appealing as this newcomer.

"So, even if Lola—that's the zebra's name—didn't have arthritis, you still couldn't ride her. She's wild."

"But why do you have wild animals?" Eddie asked.

"Because Lola and Lollipop, her friend, used to work in a small circus where they pulled a chariot. They went round and round the ring for many years until they got too old. They didn't have anywhere else to go, so they came to live with me and the other animals. Now they can eat grass and have a nice retirement."

"Just like Grandpa Whitaker moved to Hilton Head."

Kate suppressed a laugh. Her father wouldn't take kindly to his lifestyle being compared to that of two aging zebras, especially with his younger wife, his golf games and tennis matches. "Sort of, but don't tell him that."

"Okay. I'm ready to go home now."

Kate stood and took Eddie's hand. "Are you sure you don't mind taking us home?" she asked Luke.

"No, as long as your brother doesn't come after me."

"Why would you say that?"

"He doesn't like me."

"He's overprotective and he doesn't know you."

Luke's eyebrows rose as if asking, "And you do?"

Kate shrugged at the unspoken question and led Eddie toward the door. "Whatever Travis says, I'm grateful for your help. I couldn't have gotten Eddie here so quickly or easily without you."

"I'm glad I was home."

Kate paused as he unlocked the truck. "I hope we didn't interrupt your visitors…again."

"No, they're gone."

Good, she felt like saying, but she didn't. She absolutely refused to be petty, especially about a man she barely knew.

She helped Eddie into the seat and buckled him up. "I'm sure you're very busy, though." Although Luke had been much nicer and more concerned than she would have expected, he had his own life to lead.

She knew so little about him. She'd imagined much more about him than she should have, first thinking him self-possessed to the point of arrogance. In reality, he was very nice. Perhaps even a little shy. And awfully concerned about Eddie, instead of being angry.

Which made him even more endearing. Darn it. She didn't need this. Her responsibility to provide for herself and Eddie, combined with her need to stand on her own two feet for the first time, made having any interest in a man a very bad idea. And when she did decide to date again, she would be smart to start with someone less exciting and tempting than Luke Simon.

She definitely needed dating training wheels, not a wild ride on a Harley.

Luke paused after inserting the key, his look again pensive. "It's not so much that I'm busy. I've got some things on my mind."

"I'm sorry to be such a bother."

"You're not a bother. That's not what I meant."

"Still—"

"Don't worry about it," he said, cranking the engine. He put the truck in reverse and turned to look behind him, then paused and watched her intently. "I'm working on a solution," he said before driving toward the ranch.

Chapter Four

Luke straightened the collar of his white cotton shirt, the only one in his closet that was pressed. He'd waited a whole day to come to see Eddie, hoping the little boy was feeling better, and that Kate wouldn't hold a grudge against Luke or his zebra.

She could be the answer to all his problems.

She was a mother, an elementary school teacher and a woman with a lot of class. If anyone could help him clean up his act, Kate Wooten was the one. She could explain what toys a little girl would like, what sorts of things weren't safe for kids, what kind of behavior was proper and how he needed to decorate the house. So much to learn, so little time before he needed approval to take custody of Brittany.

But as much as he wanted to get his plan in action, he didn't think he should come right out and ask Kate for help. For one thing, she didn't know him very well. Until Eddie tried to ride a zebra, Kate had seemed a bit...standoffish. He'd assumed she was snobby, but maybe she was just unsure of him, his animals and his ranch. Mostly him.

Even though he didn't have much time, she needed to feel more comfortable around him first. He hoped he could make a good impression today, and move quickly to gain her cooperation. Brittany was expecting him to be her father in more than name only. They'd talked on the phone several times, and she was already making plans. Already telling him her wishes for the future.

He felt overwhelmed by the hopes of an eight-year-old.

He opened the door of his pickup, looking up toward the garage apartment, feeling as though he'd "come calling," one of the lines of dialogue he remembered from a Western film. He snatched the small bag he'd brought for Eddie from the seat and stepped out.

At that moment Travis's wife, Jodie, came out the back door of their house onto the wooden deck running halfway to the garage. In her arms she held a baby, maybe six months old. Luke remembered hearing that Jodie Marsh Whitaker was a famous model. Right now she looked very ordinary in a good way, dressed in jeans and a pink sweatshirt, her blond hair in a ponytail.

"Hello, Mr. Simon," she greeted him with a smile. "Are you here to see Kate?"

"Luke, please, Mrs. Whitaker."

She laughed. "Jodie, please."

He grinned despite his intention not to warm up to Travis Whitaker's family. "Jodie, then." He shut the truck's door and took a step toward the deck. "I came to check on Eddie."

"He's doing fine, but he has a heck of a bruise."

"I'm sure he does."

"How's the zebra?"

"Seems to be fine."

Jodie nodded, shifting the baby on her hip. "I'm sure Kate is home. Why don't you go on up? She lives over the garage for now. Just until she gets back on her feet."

Ah, yes. The divorce. "Thanks, Jodie." Before he turned away, he saw her husband exit the house and stand behind her on the deck, arms crossed over his chest. Travis was a big guy, one Luke wouldn't want to cross—unless he had to. He wasn't sure why Travis didn't like him, but Luke wouldn't let that stop him from visiting Kate or putting his plan into action.

Luke had been in a Western movie once, stunting for an actor who could barely sit a horse. He'd worn a hat pulled low, and the director had used a camera angle that hid his face. One of his scenes required him to tip that hat in the fine cowboy tradition, then spur the horse into a gallop. He wished he had that hat on now. The tip would be just what was needed to make a snappy exit.

Instead, with a somber nod toward the man scowling at him, Luke headed for the second-floor apartment.

He jogged up the stairs, not bothering to keep his

footsteps light. As a matter of fact, he hoped Kate heard him. He didn't want to surprise her, although he supposed he was the last person she'd expect to see on her doorstep.

Sure enough, she opened the glass storm door before he knocked. She was dressed in what he thought of as "schoolmarm" clothes: a fancy embroidered T-shirt tucked into a modest skirt. Not exactly sexy, but that's not what he needed from Kate Wooten.

She held the door wide, then looked past him to the couple on the patio. Luke wondered if she'd keep him out because of her brother's obvious disapproval. But then she made eye contact with Luke and smiled slightly, stepping out of the way.

"Please, come in."

"Thanks." He stepped into the living area of the apartment and was struck by how nice it appeared. All clean and bright, with creamy walls and a mix of furniture. Some pieces didn't match, but overall, the effect was…charming. Not that he knew much about decor.

"How's Eddie?"

"He's doing well. Jodie watched him today." Kate stood in front of Luke, her hands clasped in the folds of her skirt. "I'm substituting this week and next."

Luke nodded. "I'm glad he's doing okay." He felt a little nervous under her scrutiny, so he looked around some more. "Nice place."

"Travis designed it, of course, but some of the

furniture is mine." She shrugged. "What I kept after the divorce."

Luke didn't know what to say to that, so he held out the sack. "This is for Eddie."

"Would you like to give it to him? I made him lie down and rest about a half hour ago, but I doubt he's sleeping."

"Well, sure, I suppose." Now that the crisis was over and so much depended on getting Kate's cooperation, he felt a little tongue-tied around both her and her son.

"Come on back."

He followed her, watching her hips sway slightly beneath the sensible denim skirt. She wore flats, which made her considerably shorter than his own six-foot height. Her head would tuck right under his chin, and his arms wouldn't have any problems wrapping around her.

Stop thinking of her as a woman, he told himself again. She's a mother, a schoolteacher and your ticket to getting custody of your daughter.

Eddie lay on his stomach, looking at a book with dinosaur illustrations. He glanced up but didn't smile, appearing much more cautious than Luke thought a six-year-old should.

"How are you feeling, Eddie?" Luke asked.

"Pretty good," the boy said carefully, rolling to his "good" side. "Am I in trouble?"

"No, ah, this is for you." Luke handed him the bag.

The boy glanced at his mother, who nodded and smiled. Then he sat up and ripped into the paper, searching through the tissue that the salesclerk had insisted was necessary.

"Oh, wow, a zebra!"

Luke had found the small resin sculpture in the gift section of the antique shop downtown. It was owned by the wife of the Ranger Springs chief of police, but nowadays, one of her employees ran it because she'd also recently had a baby. There seemed to be a rash of babies around town, including Hank and Gwendolyn's little one.

He sure hoped it wasn't catching. Although, come to think of it, just after moving to town he found out he was a father. So maybe there *was* something in the water...

"How beautiful!" Kate exclaimed. "It looks so lifelike."

"But it doesn't buck," Luke said, smiling at Eddie.

The little boy's grin faded. "Is Lola okay? Did she get all sore in her knobby knees?"

"I think she's okay. I gave her a little extra grain last night and told her you were sorry."

"That's good. I don't want her to be mad at me."

"I don't think zebras hold grudges."

He talked to Eddie for another couple of minutes, then told the little boy he'd see him another time, but not out in the pasture and not uninvited. He sure hoped Eddie understood now that his walking around unsupervised was dangerous.

"Would you like to sit awhile?" Kate asked as they returned to the living room.

"That would be good." He took a seat in a well-worn leather armchair.

She looked at him with a perplexed expression. Okay, maybe he wasn't the most socially skilled person she'd met, but he hadn't had a lot of experience chitchatting with attractive schoolteachers. Friendly women in dark, smoky honky-tonks, now that was a different story.

"Would you like something to drink? I believe I have some iced tea made."

"No, thanks, anyway. Actually, I wanted to offer something. Kind of an apology for Eddie getting hurt."

"That wasn't your fault! I'm just glad he wasn't injured any more seriously, and that he didn't hurt your animals. I was very touched by your story of the zebras."

"Yeah, well, a lot of the animals I've taken in had a pretty tough life."

"That's very admirable that you're doing something. I mean, a lot of people would care, but not take action."

He shifted uncomfortably in the chair, wishing he'd accepted the tea she'd offered so he'd have something to do besides look at Kate. "So, anyway, I got to thinking about how Eddie likes the animals and I thought maybe some of the students at the elementary school where you're teaching would like to see them too."

She tilted her head. "What did you have in mind?"

"Kind of a minicarnival. I wouldn't bring the zebras, but the two ponies are very tame and safe, and

I have a couple of dogs that love to entertain, especially children."

"That's very generous. And not necessary, I assure you. I'm really not blaming you for any of this. You were more…well, you were so helpful by taking us to the clinic yesterday."

"It was the least I could do, since Eddie was hurt on my property."

"I'm just saying that you shouldn't feel responsible."

He frowned, concerned that she wouldn't accept his offer. He hoped she wasn't one of those women who wanted to argue about everything. "I don't have to feel responsible to want to do something nice."

She looked surprised, then said, "Of course not."

"So what do you think? Would the children enjoy it?"

"Yes, I'm sure they would. I'd have to get it approved by the principal."

"Sure. I wouldn't want to get you in trouble."

Kate stared at Luke for a moment, ideas of how he could "get her in trouble" popping unwanted into her head. Most of those ideas involved both of them being partially undressed and pressed close together. She wouldn't allow herself to go any further. Her heart probably couldn't stand a more vivid imagination.

She really had to stop thinking about him in such inappropriate ways. If she didn't have a child, if she didn't live with her overprotective brother, if she weren't a schoolteacher in a small town, then perhaps… But no, they were like oil and water, and besides, she wasn't a good judge of men. She shouldn't, she couldn't, have any kind of romantic relationship with Luke Simon.

Even if he did tempt her beyond belief.

"I'll ask and give you a call, if that's okay."

He nodded. "I'm leaving town tomorrow morning for a few days. I'll be back late Sunday, so just leave me a message if I'm not available."

She wondered where he was going. Probably a hot date. Maybe with one of those women who'd visited a couple of days ago.

"Who takes care of your animals when you leave?" she asked casually.

"I haven't had to leave before, but something just came up, something I have to take care of right away," he said. "I have someone who helps out during the days. He'll be there, plus my friend Hank will be supervising."

"Oh, I see." It didn't sound like a hot date. More like a business or personal problem. Kate knew she shouldn't feel relieved, but she did.

"Well," he said, rising from the chair, "just let me know about bringing the animals to the school."

"I will," Kate replied, getting up from the couch. "And thank you again for the present for Eddie. That was very sweet."

He appeared embarrassed by her compliment. Again, she was taken aback by Luke's shyness. She'd assumed "bad boys" would be so self-confident they'd accept praise as their due. He wasn't like that at all. He cared—about unwanted animals and curious little boys.

He was at the front door when he muttered something that sounded like "you're welcome." As a matter of fact, he looked relieved to be leaving. She probably made him uncomfortable because she was so different from the women he was accustomed to. Those women probably had lots of witty things to say, plus they knew how to flirt.

If she'd ever known how, she'd lost the ability many years ago. She'd never had to flirt with Ed Wooten. She'd certainly never strayed during their eight-year marriage. And even if she did decide to play the femme fatale, she wouldn't attempt it with Luke Simon.

"Have a nice trip."

He nodded. "I hope so." He looked far into the distance, pensive and withdrawn. "I sure hope so."

LUKE SETTLED CLOSER to the window, avoiding the tilting passenger in the middle seat who'd been dozing off and on ever since they'd taken off from Orlando. The guy reeked of beer and smelled like bratwurst when he snored. So much for enjoying the flight.

His visit with Brittany and her uncle, Andy Jacobs, had gone as well as could be expected, considering Luke had never met her and was as nervous as hell. He hadn't wanted Brittany to sense that he was on the edge of panic, because she might think he didn't want her, which was untrue.

He just wasn't sure how to be a great dad. It wasn't like he'd had a role model. It wasn't like he'd ever known his father, except his name and where he lived…with his legitimate family.

Luke pushed his negative thoughts aside. Apparently, Brittany had known about him all along. Not his real name or anything current, of course, because Shawna hadn't been able to find him. The last she knew, he was an assistant trainer and doing some B-movie stunts. He'd moved on to become a trainer and a wrangler for several larger films, and he'd specialized in riding stunts. He loved horses, mules, burros—anything with four legs and hooves.

Brittany seemed to share his love of animals. She'd shown him her collection of plush bears, dogs and pigs. She especially liked pigs. He'd get her one. Rescue groups were always looking for good homes for potbellied and half-potbellied pigs. He'd get on that Monday morning, right after he checked in with Kate about the minicarnival.

He was still in awe of his daughter. She was a shy girl who looked just like the photo her uncle had sent. She would probably need braces, if her crooked lower teeth were any indication. And she would need to feel welcome in Texas, because she had a lot of misgivings about leaving her home. She and her mother had lived with Andy ever since Brittany was a toddler.

She wasn't overly close to her uncle, Luke sensed, but she did cling to him as her only living relative. He'd promised to visit while driving his new route,

Los Angeles to Atlanta, so they could keep in touch. Luke hoped Andy kept his word. He'd seen too many good intentions vanish in the reality of life.

But he couldn't control Andy Jacobs, just like he hadn't kept his mother from loving the man who'd impregnated her and then broken her heart. He'd just have to do everything in his power to make Brittany feel welcome and loved at the ranch.

He'd created a safe, calm home for unwanted animals. Now he had an almost homeless daughter who needed to heal from her mother's death and her uncle's desertion. At least, from Brittany's point of view he seemed to be deserting her. Luke wanted to give Andy the benefit of the doubt, believing he had the right to pursue his career, his livelihood, without being burdened by his sister's child. Especially when she had a father who was willing and able to provide a home.

If he could just get approved. If he could just make his daughter feel welcome…

Which brought him back to Kate. He would continue to be as charming as possible—not a natural feat for him—and present his case that she was the best person for this job. Now that he'd met Brittany, he could also impress upon Kate how much a special little girl needed her.

He wasn't above pulling at her heartstrings to achieve his goals. He couldn't afford the luxury of being noble. Brittany had become his primary concern. Not the animals. Not his intriguing, attractive neighbor. He was a father now, and he had to start acting like one.

KATE ENTERED the teachers' lounge and headed for the refrigerator. She'd fixed herself a sandwich earlier when she'd made Eddie's lunch, and she had just enough time to put her feet up, drink some of her favorite pink lemonade and eat before getting back to her classroom.

She wasn't used to having a room full of children all day long. She'd get in the habit, of course, since she hoped to have a regular teaching job by fall. But right now, she was drained from the constant attention to all her students—their questions and comments, their actions and potential problems.

"Tired?" her fellow third-grade teacher Beverly Randolph asked as she headed for the microwave oven.

"A little, although not as much as last week. I'll be glad when Nancy comes back to work, though. This assignment has been a crash course in classroom management."

Beverly laughed. "Third-graders are a handful."

"Tell me about it. At least I have a first-grader at home. If he were older, my hair would already be turning gray." *Especially if he continued to stray from home.*

"I think you're a long way away from gray."

Not as long as you might think, Kate thought. She was thirty-two. She'd soon be past childbearing age, slipping into middle age as her son grew taller and sassier, no doubt.

She sighed, not wanting to go there. She wasn't by nature a pessimist. If she were, she would have been more suspicious of Ed, his schemes and infidelity. But she wouldn't want to go there, either. She was just tired, she told herself, and the students were restless, ready for the spring break.

They could all use a distraction. "Beverly, what do you think Mrs. Johnson would say about my neighbor, Luke Simon, bringing some performing animals to school to entertain the class? He suggested it the other day."

"Really? What kind of animals?"

"Some ponies and maybe dogs that do tricks."

"Sounds like fun!"

"So you think she might go for it?"

"You'd need to get some releases signed and make sure none of the parents had objections."

"That's all?"

"Pretty much." Beverly placed her microwaved meal on the coffee table in front of the sofa and smiled at Kate. "So, why is your new neighbor being so nice? I thought he was rather reclusive. Hardly anyone has seen him around except when he goes to the feed store, hardware store, or someplace else that's functional, not fun." Beverly smiled over her steaming meal. "And believe me, a lot of the single women have been looking for him to cut loose."

Kate shrugged, ignoring the last comment. "My son, Eddie, has been going over the fence to his property on a fairly regular basis. Last week he tried to ride a zebra and got bruised when he fell off. Luke, er, my neighbor, feels responsible, although I told him it was Eddie's fault."

"Hmm, from what I've seen of your new neighbor, he's a real hunk."

Kate shrugged again. "He's an attractive man, I suppose."

"You suppose? That man is drop-dead gorgeous."

"Who is?" Amanda Peterson, a fourth-grade teacher, asked, bringing her own lunch to the gathering.

"Luke Simon, Kate's hunky neighbor," Beverly answered.

"He's really very nice," Kate said.

"Oh, I'm sure he is. Nice on the eye," Amanda said with a laugh.

Kate didn't like the turn of this conversation. She wasn't used to women talking about men as though they were objects. She'd missed the whole *Sex and the City* era while she was married to Ed.

"So, Beverly, you think the carnival will be okay with Mrs. Johnson? I wouldn't want to bring it up if I knew she'd object, especially since I'm only a substitute."

"I think she'd love it, as long as he can assure the children will be safe." Beverly smiled at Nancy. "The question is, will Kate be safe from Luke?"

Kate felt herself blush, not a common occurrence. "He's not interested in me that way."

"Really? And why not?"

"Because I've seen the kind of women he's used

to—hard bodies and big hair. I'm not in the same league."

"You don't know that. Maybe he's tired of his normal type. Besides, you're no slouch. Just get some sexy—"

"No, I'm not going to make a fool of myself for a man. As they say, been there and done that."

Amanda leaned close. "Kate, for that man, I'd make an exception."

Beverly laughed and Kate forced a smile, but inside she knew her friends were wrong. Luke wasn't attracted to her. No, he was just trying to be friendly. A man could be nice with no ulterior motive. Couldn't he?

Chapter Five

Luke pushed open the door of the Four Square Café, searching for Hank's familiar face among the other folks having breakfast. The bell continued to jingle as he paused beside the front counter where an old-fashioned register sat next to colorful candy and mints that tempted the child in everyone.

Everyone seemed to be staring at him, which he tried to ignore. He didn't know these people—although maybe he should get around to meeting them—and besides, they still looked at him as a stranger, an outsider. Maybe that pushed too many of his buttons, since he'd been the new guy most of his life. He'd moved around a lot. He didn't have much experience settling down.

And now he had Brittany to consider…

"Luke," Hank called from a red vinyl booth halfway to the kitchen in the rear.

He headed back, trying to look friendly as he passed tables where mostly men sipped coffee. He recognized Jimmy Mack Branson from the hardware store, sitting with two other men, and Luke said hello as he went by.

"How was the trip?" Hank asked as Luke slid into the booth.

"Good. A little stressful."

"What did you think of Brittany?"

"She's great. It's kind of overwhelming, thinking she's my daughter."

"So, is she?"

"We had blood tests done, and I'll get the results back next week, but yeah, I'm pretty sure. I mean, she looks a little like Shawna, but I see myself in her, too. And the timing is right. I don't think Shawna was sleeping around with different guys. I remember her as nice, and she was real sympathetic with my mother's death."

"Well, then you're going ahead with the renovations?"

"I've got that scheduled for next week too. Getting the house up to code is one thing, but making it acceptable for a little girl is something else entirely."

"Surely she'll realize you hadn't planned—"

"I don't want to put her in that position. I want her to feel welcome."

"Of course you do, but you can't work miracles."

"I can try."

Hank grinned as though saying, "good luck."

"Besides, it's not just Brittany. It's the child services people I have to worry about. If they don't agree that I'm a suitable father, she'll be in trouble. Her uncle is leaving for his new job and she'd become a ward of the state of Florida. I'm not going to let that happen."

"If you're her father, they'll approve you. There's nothin' wrong with you. Well, you take that strong silent type to the extreme, but that's not an anti-Dad flaw. You just need to learn to loosen up."

"Hell, Hank, I'll never be as loose as you."

"We can't all be perfect," he said with a laugh.

They ordered from a waitress Hank said was new, then sipped coffee and caught up on the cutting horses Hank was training. He'd done some training for folks in the movie industry a few years back, which was when they met in California. Luke missed riding and thought about getting some pleasure horses. He'd teach Brittany, of course.

Maybe he'd even ask Eddie Wooten if he'd like to learn with her. The boy was younger, but Brittany might have fun with him. Eddie sure liked animals, and so he and Brittany had that in common.

Charlene brought out their food. "How are you boys doing?" she asked with a smile.

"Good, Ms. Jacks," Hank said with one of his big grins. He was a charmer. Back when he and Luke had been single and in California for a while, when they'd gone out on the town, the women had gravitated to Hank first because of his good looks, big grin and Texas accent. Not that Luke was complaining. He got his share of attention.

"Luke, how are those animals of yours adapting to Texas?"

"They're just fine, Ms. Jacks."

"I heard about that incident with Travis's nephew and your zebra." She shook her head as she placed scrambled eggs and Canadian bacon in front of him. "That boy has got to stay on his side of the fence."

He hoped Charlene Jacks didn't mean that she—and the rest of the town—thought his animals were dangerous. They weren't, as long as their needs were respected. "I think maybe this time he learned his lesson."

"I sure hope so. Kate's a good mother, but he's a slippery little devil."

Luke chuckled at the description, trying to relax. "I'm sure she's doing her best."

"I think so. She sure is nice. And so pretty, too." Charlene nudged Hank's shoulder. "Don't you think so, Hank?"

"Are you tryin' to get me in trouble with Lady Wendy?"

They all laughed at that, and the café owner left them to their breakfast.

"Is it just me, or is she matchmaking?"

"Of course she's matchmaking. It's the town pastime."

Luke shook his head. "I don't need that kind of complication in my life right now."

"But maybe later?"

"That's not what I meant."

"Kate is a great lady."

"Yeah, I know." He swallowed a bite of toast. "That's why I'm asking her to help me get the house ready for Brittany."

Hank placed his knife and fork on the plate and raised his eyebrows. "Really?"

"Yeah, really. I need help, and she seems to be the best person."

"I didn't think you knew her very well."

Luke placed his elbows on the table and leaned forward. "I don't know her well, but what I know says she's got all the qualifications. She's educated about kids because she's a teacher, plus she has her own son, and she's only substitute teaching right now anyway."

"Plus she's single and pretty, like Charlene said."

Luke moved back against the booth. "That's irrelevant, except it means she has a little more time, and I think she could use the money." Maybe if he told himself often enough that he wasn't interested in Kate except as someone who could help him get custody of Brittany, he'd quit thinking of her as a woman.

"You've given this a lot of thought."

"I had to come up with a plan. Getting the house— and me, for that matter—ready for Brittany is all up to Kate." Luke paused, then confided, "You know, Hank, the crazy thing is that I started this ranch to give animals a safe place. Now I've got to make it into a home for a little girl."

"Everyone deserves a home."

Luke shrugged. "I suppose. This is the first one I've ever owned."

"True. And that says a lot about you."

"What do you mean?"

"Just that you picked a small town where you didn't know anyone but me to make your home. A permanent home."

"Hey, the price of the land was right and the climate was perfect for the animals I wanted."

"Sure, but there's more to the town than the geography."

He didn't understand Hank's point. "I suppose. Mostly, I'm glad Kate is living here so she can help me. Without her, it would be overwhelming."

"How does she feel about this big task?"

Luke took a deep breath. "She doesn't know… yet."

CHILDREN HERALDED the minicarnival as a huge success. The prancing ponies and lively Jack Russell terriers gave them something to laugh about. They mimicked the animals' movements until they fell on the grass, giggling. Kate leaned against the brick wall of the school building and smiled at the joy Luke's gift gave to her class.

Her students would be the envy of the school when word got around, although she wouldn't be there to hear it. Today was her last day subbing.

"You look tired," Luke said as he walked over to her, leading the two Shetland ponies, who sported purple ostrich feather headdresses attached to their bridles. He'd already put the terriers in the truck.

"I am. But the week's over and I don't have any

big plans for the weekend, so I can rest up. Besides, I'm finished with this substitute teaching assignment. The regular teacher will be back in the classroom on Monday."

He stopped in front of her, in the shade of the building, and removed his cowboy hat. "If you don't have any plans, can I take you to dinner tomorrow night?"

Dinner? Where had that come from? And just when she'd convinced herself that he didn't—and never would—like her *that way.*

"I...I don't know what to say."

Luke shrugged. "I thought you and Eddie might want to go out. I know you have family here, but we're both kind of new to the area."

Oh, he'd included Eddie. Maybe that meant Luke wasn't interested in her as a *date.* "That's true," she said cautiously, looking from him to the children sitting beneath the only tree on the playground, sipping their afternoon juice.

The ponies shifted, drawing his attention away from her, for which she was thankful, because she didn't know what else to say to him.

"I haven't gone out much since the divorce," she finally said when the animals had settled down to crop grass beside them.

"I don't know about you, but I'm tired of eating alone," he said, stepping closer. His arm brushed hers, putting her senses on alert. His skin felt hot from the sun and so male that she nearly gasped. How long had it been since she'd been this close to a man? Other than her brother, of course, who didn't count. She couldn't remember the last time she'd felt anything from a casual contact. Maybe in the first days of her marriage. Maybe not even then.

"You're...you're what?" she managed to whisper.

"I'd like to share a meal with someone who can talk. Someone who doesn't bark or neigh or cackle."

He was lonely! "Oh. Well, of course you would." She almost felt the thoughts turning in her brain. "Why don't you come for dinner tomorrow at my place?"

"You don't have to cook for me."

"I know, but it's been ages since I've prepared a meal for another adult." Kate smiled. "I'd enjoy eating dinner with someone who didn't hide his veggies under a slice of bread, or drum his feet against the rungs of the chair."

"Hmm. I don't do either of those things."

She smiled. "I didn't think you did."

His own smile faded. "Seriously, I'm not sure your brother would appreciate my presence at your apartment."

Kate shook her head. "He's just overprotective. He thinks I'm still upset about the divorce."

"Aren't you?"

Kate scuffed her shoe in the soft dirt. "No, although occasionally I'm angry. It's been months. I'm getting on with my life."

"Yes, I can see you are."

An awkward silence descended as he watched her and she stared back, and the sounds of the schoolyard faded away. For just a moment she thought perhaps he could see her as something other than the mother of a nuisance or the sister of an unfriendly neighbor. But then she shook her head and remembered that she didn't want him thinking of her that way...as if he ever would.

"What's wrong?"

"Nothing. I should get my class inside and remind them of their reading for the weekend."

"And I should get my animals home. They're not used to performing anymore and they're too old to be out long."

"Sure." She shifted her weight and moved slightly away from his disturbing presence.

He looked at her a few more seconds, then said, "I appreciate the offer of a home-cooked meal, but I don't want to get you in trouble with your brother. Most of all, I don't want him showing up while we're eating."

"He wouldn't... Well, maybe you have a point."

"I've heard good things about the Mexican restaurant out on the state highway. Would Eddie enjoy that?"

"Yes, he would. He loves enchiladas and tacos."

"What time?"

She couldn't believe she was agreeing to go to dinner with Luke Simon. "Six o'clock? I don't like Eddie to eat and go directly to bed, so we tend to have our meals a little early."

"Even on the weekends?"

"It's important to keep a regular schedule for children," she said, maybe a little defensively.

He smiled quite unexpectedly. "See, I didn't realize that. I didn't know that keeping schedules was important."

She tilted her head. "Why would you? You're single."

"Exactly," he said, his smile fading. "So, six o'clock tomorrow." He adjusted the lead ropes for the two ponies. "Will Travis be upset if I pick you up?"

"I'm not going to worry about that. Besides, I think he and Jodie are having dinner with Hank and Gwendolyn."

He grinned. "I never thought I'd feel like a teenager who sneaked around to go on a date."

She straightened, hoping alarm didn't show on her face. "But this isn't really a date. I mean, this is about two neighbors, two newcomers, eating together." She was talking too fast, but couldn't stop herself. "I know that you're probably lonely because you've recently moved to town, and you don't know many people yet."

He looked at her oddly. "I didn't mean to upset you."

"You didn't. Of course you didn't."

"Okay, then." He drew in a deep breath, which accented his wide chest and flat stomach. "I'll see you tomorrow."

"Okay, if you're sure."

He nodded, looked at her intently again, then led the ponies to the trailer hitched to his pickup.

Kate turned away from the sight of Luke Simon's rear in those soft, faded, butt-hugging jeans. She was going to dinner with him, but it wasn't a date. He wasn't interested in her that way. He was simply lonely.

She sighed and cupped her hands around her mouth. "Come on, kids! Time to go inside."

LUKE STEERED around the town square, well satisfied with the day so far. Repairs on the house were going well, with new drywall and plumbing nearly complete. He had state-of-the-art appliances ready to be installed once the kitchen floor was finished. And he'd made a "date" with Kate—and Eddie—for dinner. One more chance to convince her he was a good guy who deserved her help.

He only hoped she'd consider his offer with an open mind. Kate was probably one of those great homemakers who baked cookies and decorated for all the holidays. He knew she was a wonderful mother, even if she had been temporarily scatter-brained when Eddie hurt himself.

She knew all those woman things that were a mystery to most men. She had class and sensitivity, plus the training to relate to children.

He'd show her Brittany's photo and ask Kate to help her adjust to life in Texas, with a father she didn't know. He had to be careful though, because he didn't want to seem too calculated. At the same time, he didn't want to reveal his panic over gaining an eight-year-old daughter.

He was doing this for Brittany, not for himself, and for her, he could do almost anything. He may not have known about her when she was born, or when she was growing up, or when she lost her mother, but he'd make it up to her. He'd be the best dad possible, even if he wasn't exactly sure what that meant…yet.

AFTER EDDIE WENT to bed, Kate called Jodie at the main house and asked her to meet her outside on the balcony. Since the divorce and move to Ranger Springs, Kate felt much closer to her sister-in-law— sometimes closer than she felt to her brother. He was, after all, a typical big brother, who always thought he knew what was best for her. Jodie, on the other hand, listened. Besides, they could "girl talk."

"What's up?" she asked, bounding up the stairs.

Kate paced across the small wood deck, feeling the nervous energy bubble up inside. "I've been asked out to dinner tomorrow. Actually, he asked Eddie and me out to dinner."

"He, who?"

"Luke Simon."

"Oh. Wow."

"It's not really a date."

"Sounds like a date. Two single people and a meal."

"And a six-year-old."

"Okay, that's a twist. But still, he asked you out."

"Should I go?"

"Do you like him?"

"Well, as a friend, I suppose. He's a lot nicer than

I thought at first, when Eddie kept going over there and bothering Luke's animals. But really, I'm not getting involved romantically with anyone."

"Right."

"It's just that Luke was great when Eddie was injured."

"Yes," Jodie said, her expression showing amusement. "I believe you mentioned that once or twice."

"I did?" Kate didn't realize she'd been talking about him much, but apparently she had. "Anyway, I think he's kind of lonely. I know he's friends with Hank, but I don't think he's socialized much around town."

"No, he's gotten a reputation as being rather reclusive."

"I think he's shy."

"Really? You'd expect a guy that good-looking wouldn't be shy."

"He's not arrogant."

"No, I didn't mean that he was. But you have to admit, when he strolled into the Four Square Café that first time, he seemed awfully confident."

"Yes. But when you talk to him, he's a little less certain of himself than I once assumed."

"Okay, so he's great looking and has a shy charm you find fascinating. And you're asking about going out to dinner with him…why?"

Kate whirled and paced back across the deck. "I'm having second thoughts."

Jodie grasped her shoulders and stopped Kate in her tracks. "About Luke, or about you?"

In a little voice, Kate answered, "Me, I think."

"Well, at least you're being honest with yourself. Have you already given him your answer?"

"I told him 'yes' earlier today at the school, when he brought his animals over."

"So there! Just go out with him and see what happens."

"But with Eddie along, it's not really a date, right?"

"If that's what you want to tell yourself," Jodie said with a smile, "you go right ahead."

Chapter Six

Kate's dilemma concerning whether she and Luke were on a real date continued as they left in his powerful truck. She told herself they were simply friends even as she stole glances at him as he drove out of Ranger Springs toward the state highway. He looked rather intent on driving, perhaps even rethinking having asked her to dinner. But he was paying attention to the conversation, making comments and not ignoring her or Eddie.

With her son sitting between them, chatting away about everything from his newfound interest in wild animal behavior to his friend Pete's new puppy, there were few awkward moments. The logical part of her brain realized she barely knew Luke Simon, while the emotional part urged her to get to know him much better.

Thankfully, he didn't seem to have any idea she thought of him as anything other than a neighbor. And she wasn't going to let on that she was attracted to him. She'd never been frivolous before and at thirty-two, she wasn't about to start. Getting involved with any man was a terrible idea. Besides, she had Eddie to consider. He was her main responsibility.

At least it looked as though she would be able to provide a home for them in the fall.

"This is a celebration," she told Luke as they finished their entrées and sipped their iced tea.

"What's the occasion?" he asked.

"The principal told me yesterday that I'm going to be offered a teaching position in the next school year."

Before she'd left the school, Mrs. Johnson had called her into the office. Kate had a few continuing education credits to make up in the summer, but pending approval by the school board, she'd be teaching second grade in August.

"That's great news. Congratulations," Luke said.

Eddie frowned. "Does that mean you'll be my teacher?"

"No, sweetie. The principal will make sure you're in the other teacher's class."

"Okay, good," he said. "Can I have dessert now?"

Kate chuckled. "I thought maybe we could have dessert at home. I made brownies and got some vanilla ice cream at the grocery."

"Mmm! Brownies!"

"What about you, Luke? Do you like brownies? Otherwise, we can get some sopapillas or flan here."

"No, homemade brownies sound great."

Kate chuckled. "They're from a mix."

"Still, you baked them."

Luke called for the check and then they argued over who would pay. Kate wanted to, because that was her way of thanking Luke for bringing the animals to school, but he wanted to because…well, because he was a man.

But this wasn't a date.

"How about we split it?"

"We're already splitting it," he answered, handing the waitress a credit card. "I'm buying dinner and you're providing dessert."

Kate knew she wasn't going to win this argument, so she stopped trying. She hoped he wasn't going into debt, though. He didn't appear to be a wealthy man and, as Travis had pointed out on at least two occasions, Luke had no visible means of support. Still, dinner at this family-owned restaurant wasn't expensive, so she tried not to worry about Luke Simon's finances.

A few minutes later they walked to the pickup with Eddie skipping along in between. Kate never knew a six-year-old could be such a good buffer. Of course, she hadn't dated since her divorce, so the subject hadn't come up.

Not that this was a date.

They chatted about Luke's animals—individual stories that were sometimes poignant, sometimes sad, but all had a happy ending. He hoped to get more animals, but he was being selective because he had to care for them for the rest of their lives. He'd made contacts with several organizations and vets, letting them know he had the space for abandoned, neglected or aging horses, donkeys—pretty much anything with four legs and hooves. He even confessed to feeding some wild deer, although they were little more than nuisances to most ranchers.

Despite his initially gruff manner, he was good with children. He'd been patient with her class and conversational with Eddie, who hung on Luke's every word.

She'd have to make sure Eddie realized Luke was only their neighbor—one who couldn't be coerced into performing favors. One who couldn't be expected to come around just to chat with a six-year-old and his divorced mother.

"Thanks again for the meal," Kate said as they continued up the driveway. "Those sour cream chicken enchiladas were great."

Luke drove smoothly toward the garage apartment. The headlights were directed straight ahead, keeping the main house in darkness. Kate could almost forget that her brother lived so close.

"I enjoyed myself, too," Luke replied, pulling to a halt and placing the truck in park. "It was nice to go out for a change. I've been eating my own cooking too long."

She couldn't imagine Luke cooking, but that was probably because Ed had never set foot in the kitchen unless he was headed directly for the refrigerator. Travis hadn't cooked when they were younger, either, but he'd taken lessons after his divorce from his first wife and now was an excellent cook, much to Jodie's delight.

"Ready for dessert?" Kate asked both the guys.

"Yeah!" Eddie answered first.

"Sounds good," Luke replied.

As she led the way up the stairs, Eddie chatting to Luke behind her about how she'd made a chocolate cake for his birthday, she felt as though Luke were watching her ascend the steps. Watching her hips beneath the chino, knee-length skirt she'd worn after much deliberation. She hadn't wanted to wear her "school clothes," but she didn't want to get too dressed up, either. The Mexican restaurant was a comfortable family place.

And after all, this wasn't a date.

She unlocked the door, noticing her hand was a bit unsteady. Not too bad, considering she'd just gone to dinner with Luke Simon, which she might get teased about if—or when—her fellow teachers or friends found out.

"Eddie, why don't you sit with Mr. Simon while I get the brownies and ice cream?" She peered over her shoulder at their guest. "Would you like some coffee?"

"That would be good, if it's not too much trouble."

"Not at all."

She worked in the kitchen, putting everything except the still brewing coffee on the tray she used when she and Eddie ate on the balcony. The gurgling of the coffee maker helped soothe her nerves, and by the time she carried dessert into the living area, she knew her evening would be ending soon with nothing momentous happening. She *was* well chaperoned, and besides, Luke wasn't interested in her *that way*.

Even if it would be nice to believe he *could* think of her as something other than Eddie's mom.

"Yummy, Mommy," Eddie said, standing up and looking at the goodies on the tray.

"Let me help you," Luke said, also rising.

She didn't want to accidentally touch him, so she put the tray down slightly away from where he reached. "I've got it," she said cheerfully. "No problem."

He sat back down and frowned, as though he wanted to say something, but didn't. As though he was intentionally trying to be on his best behavior. Which seemed a bit unusual, considering this wasn't a date....

"I CAN'T BELIEVE my sister is having dinner with Luke Simon," Travis said as Hank McCauley passed the English trifle to him. "Who knows what kind of moves that guy is putting on her right this minute."

"Moves? Good gracious," Gwendolyn McCauley remarked, pouring coffee for everyone, "she's well chaperoned by her son, wouldn't you say? Besides, I think he's rather nice."

"You think everyone's nice, darlin'," Hank replied.

"I most certainly do not!"

Jodie joined in. "Gwendolyn, you have to admit you're pretty accommodating. Why, you're even friendly to those tabloid photographers who come around every now and then."

"I know they're annoying, Jodie, but I have to think they're just doing their job, obnoxious as it may be. We English seem more accustomed to those things, with the royals and all."

"Um, I'm not royal," Jodie said, taking a bit of trifle.

"You're my royal," Travis said, giving her thigh a squeeze under the table. "We're off the subject here. What about this Luke Simon and my baby sister?"

Jodie frowned. "What about him? He hasn't done anything wrong—"

"That we know about," Travis finished.

"Come on, Travis. He's my friend," Hank said. "Do you think I'd be friends with someone who was criminal, perverted or just basically a jerk?"

"Maybe you don't know him well, either."

"Maybe you're just being an overprotective big brother," Jodie said.

"Somebody has to look out for her."

"Hmm," Gwendolyn said, raising her eyebrows and thumping her index finger against her chin. "Might that be Kate's responsibility? She is a grown woman, Travis."

"She's just gotten a divorce from a real louse who was cheating on her and stealing his clients' money."

"I don't think that was ever proved," Jodie reminded him.

"Maybe not, but we know what he was doing.

And the point is, Kate didn't know a thing. She's pretty naive."

"So what you're saying is that the teacher needs education on the ways of the world?" Hank asked.

"Exactly!"

"Then I'd say she's in good hands with Luke."

Travis gave up. Why weren't his friends—even his wife—more worried that Kate was in over her head? He loved his sister, and he seemed to be the only one who knew that an experienced, Harley-riding smooth operator like Luke Simon was way too much for Kate.

LUKE TOOK BITES of brownie and ice cream in time with Kate so he wouldn't finish too quickly. He didn't want to appear as though he was in a great hurry, which in fact he was. As delicious as the dessert tasted, he wanted to talk to Kate. The more he was around her, the more convinced he was that she was perfect.

Perfect for the task of making him into a dad, that is. Perfect for making his ranch into a home.

"Can I help?" he asked when they were finished and she began to collect the plates, bowls and spoons. She placed everything neatly on the tray.

"No, you're our guest. Besides, I need to get our coffee."

"I'm really good with dirty dishes."

"Thanks for the offer, but I'll just put these in the dishwasher as soon as I get Eddie ready for bed."

"Aw, Mom, can I stay up to see the show about the sharks on the Discovery Channel?"

"Sharks right before bedtime? I'm not sure that's a good idea."

Eddie stuck out his lip in a blatant pout. "Can I watch the cartoon channel then?"

Kate crossed her arms and smiled. "I think I've just been conned. Okay, you can watch until eight o'clock, then a quick bath and off to bed."

"Okay!"

Luke used the mother-son exchange as an excuse to grab the tray and carry it into the kitchen. Kate followed him. The small area was compact and clean, much like an efficiency apartment. He'd leased enough of those in his life to recognize the space-saving layouts and generic decorating.

"Thanks," she said as he turned around. In the close quarters, she was only a couple of feet away. Closer than she'd been earlier. Closer than she'd been when he'd carried Eddie to his truck. From here, he could see Kate's gray eyes and soft, pink complexion. She appeared so natural and wholesome. Just like an elementary schoolteacher...and a mom. He wouldn't let himself think beyond that image or he wouldn't be able to talk to her about his problem.

"I've had a good time tonight, and I know Eddie did also," she said with a smile.

"I'm glad you enjoyed it." He placed his hands in his back pockets to keep from fidgeting. "If Eddie is going to be busy for a while, could we talk?"

"Talk?"

"Yeah. I've got something to ask you."

She appeared shocked, as if he'd made some outrageous statement. Well, she hadn't been thinking about and planning this moment for days, so maybe she was surprised. He couldn't wait any longer, though. Brittany needed him.

"Oh. Very well," she replied in her best schoolteacher voice. "Would you like to take our coffee out to the balcony?"

"Sure. Sounds good."

She filled their mugs, added sweetener and cream to hers, and headed for the door.

"We'll be right outside, Eddie," she said as they passed by the couch and chairs in front of the television.

"Okay," her son replied, not looking up from the colorful but strangely animated cartoon. Luke remembered a much different type of children's show, with characters resembling those in the comic books. Brittany probably liked these new cartoons, not the old fashioned kind like his favorite character, Thundarr the Barbarian.

The night was cool now that the sun had completely set. Outdoor lights, probably on a timer, illuminated the wooden balcony. Kate wandered to the railing and looked down at the pool in her brother's backyard.

"We had a pool with a hot tub at one end and a waterfall at the other," she said, speaking softly to the night. "Ed and I hardly ever swam, but Eddie loved that pool."

"I'm sure he did." Luke smiled at the image of

Eddie doing a cannonball into sparkling blue water. He made a mental note to ask whether he should install a pool for Brittany.

"Do you miss your old life?"

She seemed surprised that he'd asked such a simple question. "I miss some of it," she replied thoughtfully. "We had friends and neighbors, we took vacations that were fun. The house was beautiful," she said as she looked out over her brother's backyard, then sighed, "but it was large and took so much time to clean. I'm looking forward to getting my own, smaller place."

He hadn't thought about how it had to feel to give up almost everything she'd become used to. Giving up a lifestyle wasn't easy, and he admired her for the way she'd started over.

"I can't really say that I miss the total package. I suppose part of me knew that type of life was precarious, especially when everything is mortgaged and borrowed and dependent on financial markets. Still, I'd been brought up wanting for nothing, so part of me expected to 'have it all' forever."

"I can understand that." His life had been completely opposite, but he was sure Kate didn't want to hear about his struggling single mom and his absent father's other family. They'd had the lifestyle of Kate's family and more, and if he let himself think about it too much, he'd get bitter and angry. That wasn't what tonight was all about.

"I'm sorry," Kate said. "I'm babbling on about

myself and you obviously had something to say. What is it?"

Now that the time had come, he felt even more tongue-tied than usual. "I kind of wanted…that is, there's something important that's come up."

She waited a moment, then said, "Yes?"

"I don't know how this will sound to you." He paused and took a deep breath, wishing he faced an angry grizzly or had to fall from a galloping horse. "Last week I found out that I have an eight-year-old daughter. Brittany."

Even in the dim light of the balcony, he saw Kate's surprise. Maybe even shock.

"I take it you weren't married or you might have known about a pregnancy."

"Not even seriously involved."

"Oh."

Luke rubbed his forehead. He told Kate about Shawna and his mother's death. "I wasn't thinking clearly then. I was all of twenty-one and trying to get jobs in California. My mom and I were close, just the two of us when I was growing up."

Kate nodded. "I understand."

"Shawna didn't even know my last name. When she tried to find me, she looked for Luke Moretti. That was my mother's last name, you see." Luke paused and looked out at the trees protecting the house to the west. "I wish I would have given Shawna my phone number or address. I wish I would have thought about her maybe needing to find me."

"I'm sure you were grieving," Kate said softly.

"Yes, I was. My mother was young. She shouldn't have died so soon. One minute she was fine, the next her heart just stopped beating and she was gone. Some type of electrical problem with her heartbeat, the doctor said."

"I'm sorry."

He shook his head, returning to his story rather than dwelling on his memories. "I didn't know this at the time, but Shawna stayed in town for a while, then went to live with her brother in Florida. That's where my daughter Brittany grew up."

Kate watched him, her expression unreadable, her eyes wide and dark in the night. "What are your plans now? Are you getting back together with Shawna?"

Kate held her breath as Luke frowned. Her question had seemed reasonable. He'd cared enough about Shawna to make a baby with her. Maybe he wanted another chance.

Maybe I'm a fool to care, Kate told herself.

"Shawna? No, I thought I mentioned…Shawna died in a car accident last year."

Kate hadn't expected that, hadn't braced herself for anything so serious. "Oh, poor Brittany."

"Yeah, but she seems to be doing okay, considering."

Kate wasn't sure how his personal life affected her, but he'd wanted to talk, and now she was caught up in the story. "What are you going to do?"

"I'm bringing Brittany to Texas to live with me. Her uncle, who she's been living with, contacted me.

He's taken a job as a long-haul trucker. He can't keep her with him, and she doesn't have any other family. I'm all she's got, and really, I'm glad. I want to claim her as my daughter."

That was admirable. Many men—Ed for instance—would have insisted on paternity tests first and tried their best to get out of responsibility for an eight-year-old. "This will really change your life."

"Exactly!" he said, straightening and, in the process, moving a little closer. She didn't want him closer. She didn't want to get any ridiculous notion that he'd asked her out to talk about something...personal.

"I've never thought about children much. I've never been around them, since I'm an only child and most of my friends are single. Well, except for Hank, but he and Gwendolyn just have a baby. Not the same, really, as an eight-year-old."

"No, not at all."

"So I'm going to need some help. I have to get ready for Brittany. Plus I have to get approved by social services."

"That's understandable, especially since you don't have an ongoing relationship with her."

"I met her last week. I flew down to Florida before I brought the animals to the school."

"And how did that go?"

"As well as could be expected. We were both kind of reserved, I suppose. I'd say she's shy, though, rather than resistant to the idea of living with me."

"And how would she describe you?"

Luke looked at her a moment, then smiled. "See, that's exactly why I need your help."

Kate knew her surprise showed on her face. "*My* help? What...what are you talking about?"

Chapter Seven

Luke's smile faded. "Like I said a while ago, I'm going to need help."

Kate tried not to sputter. "I thought you meant from a professional. Like a lawyer or a social worker."

"No, I'm not worried about that. I need to learn how to be a dad, how to make my house a home. I need to understand Brittany and know what to expect from her."

"Luke, I'm a schoolteacher, not a counselor! I'm not qualified to help you."

"Of course you are. You're perfect."

"Hardly," she scoffed.

"Perfect to help me understand how to make an eight-year-old happy."

"I'm just beginning my teaching career. Right now I'm only a substitute. I'm doing good to make them behave, much less be happy."

Luke shook his head. "You're great with kids. I saw it yesterday. You know all about them, like when I asked about bedtime, and you explained being consistent."

"That's common sense."

"No, you're just used to thinking that way. Believe me, it's not common to have insight into kids. I really don't have a clue, Kate." He put his coffee mug on the railing, then captured her hands before she could step away. "You're my best hope, my only hope, to make this new relationship with Brittany work."

She ignored the shock of the sudden contact, the warmth of his hands on hers and the feel of his calluses as he held her firm. She ignored all those feelings because he wasn't holding her hands for the right reasons. He hadn't looked into her eyes because he couldn't stop himself, because he wanted her enough to defy her brother and maybe even his own convictions about not getting involved.

No, that's not why he was here with her, and the knowledge hurt more than it should have. More than was wise or even sane.

Right now, though, she needed to focus on his question. On his insistence that she could help him. "No, Luke, I'm not qualified. You don't know this, but I have a terrible relationship with my own father. And I was too blind to Ed's inadequacies to know what was going on in my life. That's not a great track record. I'm not the right person."

"Yes, you are. I need you, Kate." He stepped close enough for her to see the glistening depths of his dark eyes, the clear tan of his skin, and smell his crisp, seafresh aftershave mixed with the coffee he'd finished moments ago. "Your relationship with your father doesn't matter to me. Your husband was a jerk. I know you're a good parent, a good person. Please," he finished softly.

Kate felt her panic grow. "Luke, I'm struggling myself. I'm trying to start over and barely making ends meet with substitute teaching."

"I'll pay you enough that you won't have to substitute. Twice what you'd make teaching, if that would help."

She felt herself gape, then blinked and pulled her hands from his. "I thought you needed a *favor*."

"You mean you thought I'd expect you to do this for *free*?"

That's exactly what she'd thought. That he was appealing to her as a friend and neighbor. Not that he wanted to *hire* her to rearrange his life. Apparently she'd been wrong about a lot of things tonight.

"I'm sorry, Kate. I'm not doing a very good job explaining all this, am I?"

Of course he didn't think of her as a friend. They barely knew each other.

She almost laughed. Here she'd been concerned that this dinner…engagement might turn into a date, and in reality, it was a job interview! "No, I'm sure I just misunderstood."

"Look, I'm not accustomed to telling other people my business, much less asking them for help. But this is so important. Brittany is so important."

"There are other people more qualified than me."

He shook his head. "No one that I trust as much as I trust you. Like I said, you're perfect. You're a mother, you're a trained professional teacher and you have style. Class. That's something I don't understand, Kate. I grew up poor with a single mother. She taught me about animals and working and taking care of myself. I don't know how to be a father to a little girl."

"Oh, Luke…"

"If you don't want to do it for me, then think of Brittany. She needs me to be her father. I need you to make me into the best father I can be."

Kate closed her eyes against his entreaty. How could she say no? How could she ignore his very real plight?

She opened her eyes and looked up into his worried expression. "When is Brittany coming to live with you?"

"That's the problem. We have two weeks."

"Two weeks!"

"Yes, we'd better get busy tomorrow. When can you come over?"

AFTER PROMISING Luke she'd call him the next day to set up a schedule, then getting Eddie in bed, Kate flopped on the couch and stared at the dark TV. Of all the things she'd imagined—or been afraid to imagine—about this nondate tonight, Luke's confession that he had a daughter wasn't even on the radar.

She'd been a fool to get excited about being asked

out by a handsome, exciting and—now she realized after computing his age based on Brittany's conception—younger man. At the most, thirty years old to her own thirty-two. Not a huge age difference, but surprising. His quiet, commanding presence made her assume he was older.

She'd always felt very mature, very centered, until her own world had turned upside down. Luke apparently had been going along, unaware that he'd fathered a child. She and Luke were so different, but they'd both been through something momentous.

That didn't mean she should get involved in his life.

She was confused because of his announcement and angry at herself for thinking, just for a moment, beyond all good sense, that he might find her attractive. Womanly. This dinner and dessert had been a job interview, pure and simple.

She had no idea whether he'd be a good father or not, whether he could or would be approved by the proper social-services agencies or lawyers or whatever. She wasn't even sure she should get involved, even if she could help, which he seemed convinced she could.

She hugged one of the sofa pillows to her chest. How in the world could she succeed when she had so many doubts?

As much double-thinking as she'd done since his announcement, she kept thinking of his little girl, who'd lost the only parent she knew, who lived with her uncle who now had to give her up. Brittany didn't know Luke except for that one brief trip he'd made to Florida earlier this week. How was that poor little girl feeling, knowing she would go to live with a father she didn't know, in a new place with none of her friends?

Even so many years after Kate had done her student teaching, she remembered a little girl, about the same age as Brittany, who'd been uprooted from her home. She was quiet and shy, as Luke had said Brittany was, and she didn't interact with the other children. In turn, they'd teased her and talked about her, making her life miserable. When Kate and her supervising teacher had talked to the harried mother, they'd been told she was doing the best she could to cope. She was estranged from her own family. Her husband had left her and the children—something Kate could now identify with—and her in-laws sided with him, telling her she could leave the kids with them but they wouldn't support her. She was barely making a living on minimum wage. The children suffered from so much, but most of all, losing all the family they'd ever known.

Brittany would feel the same, Kate knew. She'd go to school at Ranger Springs Elementary with a different accent, different clothes and a new father she, not to mention the rest of the community, barely knew. The children in her class wouldn't intend to be cruel, but that would be the result. Brittany would be lost, alone and sad.

Unless Kate did something to help.

She'd have to work closely with Luke, day in and

day out. She'd look into his thickly lashed dark eyes, and her attention would be diverted every time he spoke in his rich, deep voice. How could she get anything accomplished when he made her so flustered?

She couldn't. She'd simply have to become immune to his looks and personality. Now that she knew he wasn't attracted to her, she could be sensible. Couldn't she?

She sighed, gave the pillow one more hug, then tossed it across the room. How in the world would she convince herself that Luke was simply a father who needed her help?

EARLY THE NEXT MORNING, Luke stood in the midst of the chaos of his living room, taking in the smells of drywall and joint compound, freshly cut pine boards and primer. He was just about to make a fresh pot of coffee when he heard gravel crunching on the drive outside, accompanied by the purr of an engine. He walked to the front window and looked out to see a familiar metallic blue dualie parked next to his white pickup.

"Hey, Hank," he said a moment later as his friend walked into the room.

"Quite a mess."

"It doesn't look like anything will be ready in another week, but the remodeler promised it would, and I've written a performance clause into the contract."

"Good idea, since you're in such a hurry."

"Nothing is going to keep me from being ready for inspection. And nothing is going to make me disappoint my daughter."

"You've got a long way to go."

"Yeah, I know it. Come on. I'll show you the rest." He preceded Hank down the darkened hall—the new overhead lights and sconces weren't in yet—and into the bedroom Brittany would occupy.

"I don't know what she'll like, but she has a big stuffed animal collection." He thought maybe she'd like a circus or a zoo theme for the room, but wasn't about to run that by Hank. "I was in a wealthy producer's home once and saw the kids' bedrooms. The boy's was done as a speedway, with the rear end of a car as the bed and a racetrack upside down on the ceiling. The little girl's was all pink and black Paris and poodles, with fancy furniture and fluffy feather boas. I'd like something like that for Brittany." He sensed she should be involved in the process, so maybe he did have some instincts, as Kate suggested last night.

"That's pretty fancy."

"Yeah, I don't know if it's possible. I just want her to feel welcome, you know?"

"Sure. But really, she's going to be glad to be here, don't you think?"

Luke shrugged. "I don't know. She doesn't know me...except for that one visit and my phone calls. And she's never been to Texas before."

"So is Kate helping out?"

"She said she would." Luke shook his head. "She thought I wanted her to do it as a favor. Can you believe that?"

"Well…yeah."

Luke frowned. "Why?"

"Because that's what neighbors do."

"This is a lot of work. I'd never ask someone to do this for nothing."

"She probably thought you were asking as a friend."

"We aren't *that* friendly."

"I thought maybe you were dating."

"What? Where did you get that idea?"

"From what I hear around town. Taking your animals to her school. Taking her out to dinner. And all that after saving her little boy from your rampaging zebras."

Luke scowled. "My zebras weren't rampaging. And Kate and I aren't dating."

"So you were just being friendly?"

Luke turned away. No, he'd been calculating. He'd needed Kate and he'd done what he had to do to make himself appear better so she'd help him. If folks knew, he'd look pretty bad, but he'd live with that.

If Kate thought about how he'd gotten closer to her, she might think him devious. Contemplating his situation made his head hurt more than worrying about getting his house completed on time.

"I've been friendly, but not romantic. I never did anything to make her believe I was coming on to her."

"Well, that's good," Hank said with a smile.

"I just needed her to help me get ready for my daughter."

"Whatever you say."

"I don't have time for anything else."

"Sometimes you get interested in somebody at the worst possible time, not when it's convenient."

"And you can keep from getting interested if you stay on task."

Hank grinned and shook his head. "I hope that works for you."

It had so far, but now wasn't the time to test his theory, though he had a suspicion it might be tried before the next few weeks were over.

"Look, Kate is so damn smart—everything I'm not when it comes to kids."

"Trust your instincts. You might not have formal training, but believe me, in a few months, you'll feel like a seasoned pro. You'll be a great dad."

"I'm not so sure about that." Up until now, he'd never missed going to college or having a white-collar profession. He'd worked hard with his hands and his brain, using his talent to get ahead in Hollywood. Although he'd never done anything tremendously important—except maybe to a group of misfit animals who now called the Last Chance Ranch their home—he didn't feel bad about his life, either.

Having a child changed all that. When he'd seen her photo and read that letter, he'd known his life would never be the same. The reality was just now sinking in, and along with it, fear. Gut-wrenching, bone-deep fear that he wouldn't be a good father. That he'd mess up Brittany's life forever. She didn't know him; she had no reason to trust him. What if he was such a huge disappointment that she'd never get over losing her mother, her uncle and the only home she'd known?

God, he couldn't screw this up. He had to get approved by the court. And most of all, he had to find a way to become the kind of dad Brittany would respect…and maybe someday grow to love.

"Just wait and see." Hank turned and walked back down the hall toward the front door. "And keep me updated on how your plan to avoid gettin' too *friendly* with Kate is going."

ON SUNDAY MORNING, while Eddie watched TV, Kate picked up the phone for the third time and dialed Luke's number. This time she dialed all seven digits and didn't hang up before the call went through. This time she was really going to make arrangements to go over.

He answered on the fourth ring, his voice breathless.

"Luke?"

"Hi, Kate."

"Did I catch you at a bad time?" she asked, not sure she wanted the answer.

"I was in the paddock. I ran for the phone out here in the barn."

"I…I wondered when you wanted me to come over." She'd barely slept because she'd been thinking so much about what he needed. Not as a man, but as a father.

"Anytime." She detected the anxious quality of his voice even over his deep breathing and the sounds of animals in the background.

"I can't stop thinking about Brittany. About how concerned you are about her moving here."

"I'm more than concerned. I'm worried sick. That's why I need you, Kate."

She closed her eyes against his admission. She knew instinctively that Luke wasn't the kind of man who revealed much about his feelings or his fears. She felt closer to him for the trust he'd placed in her.

"I don't know if I'm exactly who or what you need, Luke, but I can't ignore the plight of your daughter. I'll do whatever I can to help you make your house into a home."

"And make me into a father," he added.

"That one's up to you. All I can do is tell you what I know about eight-year-old girls."

"I'll take whatever you can give."

"Speaking of that, I can give you two weeks, then after spring break I need to get back to substitute teaching. I'm probably going to be offered a position and I need to make myself as available as possible. Plus, the experience is very important to me."

She heard him sigh and imagined him running his hand over his face. "I understand. That's okay. When can you come over?"

"I need to get Eddie dressed and explain to him what's going on. Do you have any problem if I tell him about Brittany?"

"Not at all. I mean, I don't guess you should go into detail about my relationship with her mother."

"No! I wouldn't do that."

"I'm sorry. Of course you wouldn't." He sighed again. "This is all new to me."

"It's new to me, too. Believe me, I've never been a consultant to a new father before."

Luke chuckled. "We're a real pair, aren't we?"

The image of the two of them, holding hands and smiling at each other, popped into her head. But they weren't a pair of anything, she told herself. "We'll be fine." *I hope,* she silently added, and crossed her fingers for luck.

After she ended the call, she told Eddie she was going to the garage to look through some boxes. She'd kept her college textbooks and student-teaching materials just in case she decided to teach once Eddie got older. Never did she think she'd be using her teaching degree while Eddie was still so young, or use her texts to help a new father.

Of course, she thought as she skipped down the steps, she'd never imagined her marriage ending either, and look what had happened as a result. She'd been caught completely off guard by Ed's perfidy.

She entered through the side door of the three-car garage and turned on the lights. Her modest compact seemed tiny in comparison to Travis's monster SUV and Jodie's elegant BMW. Jodie used to drive a snazzy little convertible out in California, but she'd traded pizzazz for safety. Besides, as she had explained, much of the time it was too hot to drive a convertible in Texas.

Kate was just glad she had air-conditioning in her little sedan. When she was a suburban "soccer mom" in Dallas, she'd driven a luxurious but sporty SUV with a DVD player in the back for Eddie and every convenience for herself. It had been repossessed just before she'd been forced to sell most of their furniture and belongings.

She'd unpacked the box and was sorting her teaching materials into subject matter when the garage door opened. She looked up into the frowning face of her brother.

"What's this I hear about you dating Luke Simon?"

"Good morning to you, too," she said flippantly.

"Is it true?"

"I'm not dating Luke Simon," she said, and went back to her books. However, she knew her answer wouldn't appease him if he was on his high horse. "Where do you get all your gossip? Have you been hanging out at the beauty shop?"

Travis snorted. "Helen said Charlene Jacks told her this morning that Carole and Greg Rafferty saw you at the Mexican restaurant last night."

Helen was Travis and Jodie's housekeeper, who was obviously in touch with everyone in town through Charlene Jacks at the Four Square Café. "I was there with Eddie and Luke, having a friendly dinner. We are not dating."

"Carole and Greg thought it looked like a date."

"Oh, give me a break. What are we, in the ninth grade?"

Travis walked over, leaned against the wall and crossed his arms over his chest. "No, unfortunately, we're all grown up. That's what I'm worried about."

"Believe me, Travis, when I say that Luke and I are not romantically involved."

"Then why did you go out to dinner with him? Good grief, Kate, if you needed to get out, you could have had dinner with us and Hank and Gwendolyn."

"Wow, that sounds like such fun. Two couples, two babies, a divorcée and her six-year-old."

"Feeling sorry for yourself? Is that what that date was about?"

"Oh, for heaven's sake! It wasn't a date, it was a job interview!"

Travis looked as stunned as she'd felt last night. "What are you talking about?"

"The reason Luke asked me to dinner, I thought, was because he was guilty about Eddie falling off the zebra. But it turns out he's got a daughter who's coming to live with him, and he needs some help getting his place ready for her."

"So why doesn't he hire Robin Parker? Why is he interviewing you?"

"Because he's worried sick about being a good father, and he believes he needs more than decorating."

Travis narrowed his eyes. "Like what?"

"Like knowing how to relate to an eight-year-old girl he just discovered is his daughter."

"He's so irresponsible that he didn't even know he had a daughter?"

"Hey, it happens to the best of men—or so I've been told."

At her jab about Travis's rushed marriage to Jodie last year, he shifted uncomfortably. "That's not the point. Why didn't he know about her for *eight years?*"

"It's a long story, and it's his to tell…or not. You'll just have to trust me when I say that Luke is a good man who is trying to do the right thing."

"He's a stranger that we know hardly anything about."

Kate put down her book with a little too much force—not that she threw it, exactly—and glared at her brother. "Leave it alone, Travis. I'm doing what I think is best."

"And I'm just trying to look out for you."

"Why?"

"Because you're my little sister and you…well, you've been through a lot."

Tears formed, but Kate tried not to show Travis that his mistrust of her abilities hurt. Deeply. "I've been through a lot because I made mistakes. That doesn't mean I'm incapable of making good decisions."

"I never said you couldn't make good decisions. I just don't think you have much experience with men like Simon."

She blinked and felt herself flush with anger. "No, I don't. My experience with men is pretty much limited to my lying, cheating ex-husband, whom I should have known was a cheat, and my overbearing older brother, who likes to point out every opportunity that I'm silly and foolish."

"Kate, that's not true. You just usually think too highly of people."

"Don't patronize me, Travis, and don't...just don't tell me what to do." She pushed the box aside and turned toward the door, ready to march up the stairs. "I'm going to help Luke Simon and I'm going to get paid for it, and come fall, I'm going to move into my own place where I can avoid all men altogether!"

Chapter Eight

Kate showed up just after lunch, a canvas tote of teaching materials and her six-year-old in tow. She wasn't about to let Eddie run off to bother the zebras, ponies or donkey again. She, Luke and Eddie were going to have to agree on some strict ground rules if she was going to be at the ranch often.

Not that talking to Eddie had done much good so far.

"Good, you're here," Luke said, walking out the door and looking relieved.

First Travis, now Luke—why couldn't men just say hello?

"If you're going to make your daughter—or anyone, for that matter—feel welcome, it's best to use some form of greeting. For example, 'Good afternoon. I'm so glad to see you today.'"

Luke stopped in his tracks and stared for a moment. Then she thought he blushed, but she wasn't sure because he was in the shadow of the porch. "I'm sorry. That was rude." He took a deep breath. "Good afternoon, Kate and Eddie. How are you today?"

Eddie waved, then turned his attention to the yapping Jack Russell terriers in their run beside the barn.

Kate said softly to Luke, "Other than having been grilled by my overbearing brother, I'm fine." In a normal voice, she added, "How are you?"

Luke winced. "I'm good, but I'm sorry Travis is giving you grief. I take it he's against your helping me."

"He's against my having dinner with you, too."

Luke leaned down and took the tote bag from her. "Word travels fast in this town."

Kate ignored the feel of his warm, firm fingers closing over hers as she relinquished her hold on the bag. "Unbelievably so, especially if anyone has visited the Four Square Café, the beauty shop, or the hardware store. Those seem to be the hotbeds of gossip."

He pulled open the door and stepped out of the way. "Would you like to come in?"

Kate smiled at him as she walked past. "Very nicely said, Mr. Simon."

"Thank you, Teacher," he said, grinning.

Her mood lightened, and she and Eddie stepped through the doorway of Luke's ranch house. The structure wasn't remarkable, just clapboard siding with a brick fireplace and a front porch wide enough for a couple of chairs. Inside, however, the place was a mess of construction. Lumber leaned against the far wall and several piles of scrap building material littered the floor. She couldn't pinpoint the odor—something damp but not moldy—and multiple paint cans were clustered in a far corner.

"Uh-oh," Eddie said, looking around. "Your house is really messy."

Kate bit her bottom lip, and Luke laughed out loud. "Yeah, it's really messy, Eddie, but in a week, it will be all finished and nice."

"Oh. Okay," her son said, looking around skeptically.

"Let me show you the bedrooms."

Kate almost stumbled on the flat concrete floors.

"Are you okay?" Luke asked, apparently unaware of the implication she'd placed on his innocent remark.

"Must have been a nail or something," she improvised. She grasped Eddie's hand firmly and forced a smile. "Lead the way."

Luke opened the first door to the left. "This is the bedroom I've been using as my office. I'm not having anything done to it."

The dull grayish-white walls had no decoration except for a tattered movie poster above a functional wood desk. A laptop rested next to a fax machine and telephone. A large desk chair in nondescript gray had been rolled away from the work area. The windows overlooked the porch and front yard, such as it was, and the pasture across the driveway.

Eddie went over and looked out. "Look, Mommy, I can see Lola and Lollipop."

"Yes, I see. Come on. Let's look at some more rooms."

"Can I go outside?" Eddie asked.

"No, absolutely not. Not right now."

Eddie poked along as Luke led them toward the next small bedroom down the hallway. "This is Brittany's room."

"Who's Brittany?" Eddie asked.

"You didn't tell him?" Luke asked Kate.

"Not her name." She knelt down. "Brittany is the little girl I told you about, Luke's daughter. She's eight years old, and she's coming to live here very soon. That's why Luke is working so hard to get everything done."

"Oh, okay. Can I play with her?"

"I'm sure you can," Kate said to her son as they stood close together in the narrow hallway.

"She'll need a friend," Luke said. "She doesn't know anyone in Ranger Springs."

"I have a friend named Pete."

"Yes," Luke said with a smile, "I remember hearing about Pete's new puppy."

"Are you getting a puppy for Brittany?"

"Uh," Luke hedged, looking at Kate, "I haven't really thought about it."

"Probably not right away," she answered. "She'll need to get settled in first. And it's not good to surprise someone until you know what kind of pets they like."

"Good answer. My mother would completely agree."

"Your mother?"

"She worked in a pet store for most of her life. And on the weekends, she also worked for a couple of trainers at a stable just outside of town. She loved animals."

"So that's where you got it."

Luke shrugged. "I've been around dogs, cats, ferrets, rats, hamsters, guinea pigs and horses all my life."

"Yes, but you chose to make them your life's work."

"I suppose. I don't know if I'm old enough to call this my life's work, at least not yet."

"Good point. You are rather young."

He looked at her strangely. "What do you mean?"

Kate shrugged. "Nothing, just that you're only what, twenty-nine?"

"Thirty, as of last February."

"Like I said, young."

"You're not any older…are you?"

"Just a little," she replied, no intention of telling him more. She might be a temporary employee, but she didn't need to tell him everything. "So, about Brittany's room?"

Luke stepped through the doorway. "It's small, but I think we can fix it up really nice for her."

Kate looked at walls the same dingy white as those in the office. "We really should call Robin Parker. She's an interior designer and owns the antique shop Robin's Nest downtown."

"Yes, I met her at the café once and I've been in her store." He looked a little uncomfortable. "I've never worked with an interior decorator before."

"I understand, but if we could get her help with the decorating, we could accomplish so much more."

"You're right. I'll call her Monday."

"If you have some ideas, I'm sure she'll be glad

to listen. After all, we all want to make this room welcoming for Brittany."

Eddie wandered off to peer into the closet.

"It's kind of hard to think of other people wishing me and my daughter well. It's a small town kind of thing, I suppose, and I've never lived anywhere like this before."

"The community is strong. If you'll let them, they'll really take you in."

"I'm not sure I'm ready for that."

Kate placed her hand on Luke's forearm and looked deep into his eyes. "Brittany will need you to be a part of the town so she can fit in better at school. She'll need friends. Little girls especially like to have friends over and visit their homes. Parents aren't going to allow that if they don't know you and feel comfortable with you supervising their children."

"It's a little early to be thinking about sleepovers and play dates. I'm still getting used to having a child."

"I understand, but your goal with Brittany is to provide stability. She needs to know you're not going to leave her, that she'll have a home no matter what."

As Kate watched Luke's face, the truth of her words sank in. *She* needed security and stability. She'd thought people weren't going to leave her, but they did. Ed left her emotionally long before he moved out physically. He deserted all the dreams and refuted all the morals she thought they shared. That's why she needed independence.

But making a home for Luke's daughter wasn't about old history, even when the memories threatened to overwhelm. "I'm sorry. I didn't mean to lecture," she said as she removed her hand from his arm, which was probably too familiar a gesture.

"You aren't. You're doing your job, teaching me about child psychology and making me into a father."

"Yes, my job. I know," she said, forcing a smile, "but still, I don't mean to sound like a know-it-all."

"You don't. You sound compassionate and…informed."

"Thank you." She looked at Eddie, who sat cross-legged on the floor, playing with some short lengths of wire and metal washers. "Eddie, let's not sit on this floor. We don't know what might be in the old carpet."

"Right," Luke said. "It's still pretty dirty, even though I vacuumed before they started working in here."

Kate had a hard time picturing Luke Simon cleaning the house. He was a bit too masculine, a bit too wild to push a vacuum cleaner. Or at least, she assumed such good-looking men didn't spend their time on domestic chores.

He showed them the small bathroom across the hall that Brittany would use, tiled in sixties two-toned green. The last room at the end of the hall was the master bedroom. When Luke opened the door, Kate felt like leaving. She really didn't want to get up close and personal with Luke's furniture and belongings. But she forced herself to stay and get acquainted with the layout of the house and the furniture he already had in case he needed her advice.

A king-size bed took up most of the floor space. He had no headboard. A comforter was pulled up over dark sheets, and at least four pillows were stacked against the wall, as though he leaned back there at night before going to sleep. A plastic storage crate served as a nightstand, holding a lamp and a book. She stepped into the room and looked at the other walls. He had a single chest of drawers, some boxes yet to unpack, and not one decorative or family item to show who lived here.

"There's a closet on that wall," he said, pointing to the closed door.

"I see. Well, your house certainly has potential."

"That's a nice way to put it. I have a functional house, one that needs lots of work. I can't do everything before Brittany comes to live with me, so we should prioritize."

"We can do that. But mostly, we have to get Brittany's space ready and make sure the house is safe."

"What's involved in making a house safe for an eight-year-old? A baby, I understand. But she's older."

"Yes, old enough to get into a lot of things. After the workers finish with cabinets and doors and painting, I can go through with you to make sure dangerous substances are stored properly and that there are no blatant dangers."

"Okay. Anything else?"

Kate took in a deep breath. "I'm not sure. I'm new at this, too."

"I'll show you the rest of the house and the grounds."

He took them through the torn-up kitchen and dining room, then out the back door. Two steps down was a path leading to the drive. The single car garage was halfway to the barn. His white pickup was parked beside the house, and a shiny new horse trailer rested behind the barn.

"I'm planning on building a larger garage with a covered walkway from the house to the barn for convenience during bad weather."

"Good idea." Everything he planned was well considered, but she wondered how he would pay for all this construction and decorating. She hoped he wasn't overextending himself at the bank to get ready for Brittany and fix up his ranch. She had no idea what a stuntman and trainer made. He didn't seem to be working any longer.

"Did you get rid of your motorcycle?"

"No, but I don't ride it much anymore."

They walked around the yard, with Luke pointing out the various pastures. New metal-post fences gleamed in the sunlight. A large pile of trimmed brush and tree limbs showed how much work he'd done to get the land ready for his animals. He'd taken care of them before himself, she realized as they walked toward the barn.

The two barking, bouncy terriers raced around the large run alongside the barn, facing the house.

She'd thought about getting a dog, but envisioned something small, furry and quiet. A dog that would curl up beside her on the couch after quietly playing ball with Eddie.

"Those are my Jack Russell terriers," Luke said, hunkering down and sticking his fingers through the chain-link fence. "They were in a small circus in Kansas, and the owner didn't have anywhere for them to go after it closed. They aren't really trained to be house pets, so I built them a big run beneath the tree, sheltered by the barn."

"They're certainly…active."

"Yes, they are. I'm going to socialize them and hope we can find them homes."

"That's good."

She walked beside Eddie, following Luke, and in a moment stepped into the spacious barn.

"This is nice," she said, looking at the new stalls and all the places where he'd repaired the structure.

"A good barn is important for animals, especially those who are elderly or infirm. I have a well-stocked supply of basic medical supplies."

"Do you keep it locked?"

"Yes, I do. Even though it's just me and my helper, Carlos, I know that people could come looking for painkillers and antibiotics."

"And children can get into things that can hurt them." She looked at Eddie, who was peering into each empty stall.

"Where are all the animals?" he asked.

"They're out in the pasture right now. They like the sunshine and fresh grass when the weather is nice."

"Do they come inside to sleep?"

"Not unless the weather is really bad."

"Does Lola come inside?"

"No, she usually stays in the pasture with Lollipop."

"Oh."

"This was a nice tour, Luke," Kate said, hoping to divert Eddie's attention from those darn zebras. "I have some materials you might want to look at, then we can get busy Monday morning."

"You're leaving so soon?"

"Not quite yet, but I can't stay too long. Eddie and I will be having Sunday dinner with Travis and Jodie," *if I'm still talking to my brother,* she silently added, "and I have some laundry to do to get ready for the week."

"Oh." He sounded so disappointed.

"I'll be back as soon as Eddie goes to school Monday."

"You get to come over and see the animals, Mommy?" Eddie asked in a plaintive, whining voice she didn't like.

"I'm working for Mr. Simon for two weeks, like I told you earlier. He needs to get ready for his daughter Brittany to come here to live."

"I know, but I could help."

"No, your job is to go to school. You'll have plenty of time to come back over and see both the animals and Brittany after we get all our work done."

He scuffed his tennis shoe in the soft dirt outside the barn and stuck his lip out just a little, but didn't protest any further as they walked back to the house. He asked permission to sit on the front porch and Kate told him okay, as long as he didn't wander off.

Luke worked at moving some items around in the living room while Kate looked through her tote bag and glanced out the door to make sure Eddie hadn't headed for the pasture.

"Here are a couple of books on children I thought would be helpful. They explain what's going on at different phases of childhood, both physically and mentally. I think this will give you some insight into Brittany, especially since you didn't get to watch her grow up."

"That's something I'll always regret."

"I'm sure you will. But you still have many years with her before she becomes an adult, so don't dwell on the past. Moving forward will help both of you, although I have to say that I think it's a mistake not to talk about anything she'd like to discuss. She may want to talk about her mother, her uncle, her friends or her school."

"Of course, although I don't know what I can say to her about them. I didn't know her mother well and I've only met her uncle once."

"She won't want answers from you, Luke," Kate said, once again wanting to reach out to touch him but controlling her impulses this time. "Mostly, she'll want you to listen."

"I hope she'll trust me enough to confide in me."

"It may take some time, but I'm sure she will. Just let her know you're willing to listen or to help her when she's ready."

"I'm going to do my best."

"I know. You're very motivated, and that's the most important thing." Kate glanced outside again, thankful that Eddie was intently watching some birds in a nearby bush.

"I still have my doubts, but with your help, I feel much more confident."

"I'm glad." Kate turned to place the rest of her items back in the tote. She'd need them later. No need to overwhelm Luke right now. "I suppose I should be going."

He stepped closer, so close she felt his warmth and smelled the detergent in his cotton shirt, mixed with his crisp aftershave. "Kate, I hope Travis isn't giving you too much grief. I honestly didn't consider how he might react when I asked you to help me. I was thinking only of myself...and Brittany, of course."

She took a small step away and turned to face him. "Of course. I understand." Taking a deep breath, she continued. "Please, don't concern yourself with my relationship with my brother. He's always been overprotective, and I'm a little sensitive right now."

"Yeah, I guess my timing is pretty bad."

"It's not that. It's just that since the divorce, I haven't dated or even made any new friends outside of Travis's circle. He's convinced I'm going to make bad choices when I branch out on my own."

"And he's already decided I'm the spawn of Satan."

"No! He just doesn't know you. He's more accustomed to people who move in and try to blend into the community. He doesn't understand why you're more private."

"Do you understand?"

She looked at him, surprised at the question. She hadn't even thought about it until now. Every time she talked to Luke, she learned more about his past, but she didn't know enough. "Not yet."

"I'm not so mysterious."

"I know, but you are private. Maybe we could work on getting people to know you better."

"Maybe. Will you help me with that, too?"

Kate nodded, distracted by his intense dark eyes, and long hair that looked as soft as silk. At this moment, she might agree to almost anything.

"Will your brother mind?"

"Mind what?"

"If you're seen around town with me."

Kate sighed, jarred out of her inappropriate thoughts. "Probably, but I'm not going to worry about him. He's got to start having faith in me. He forgets I'm an adult, not just his little sister."

Darn it, now she was all upset again, thinking about Travis, which was probably better than thinking impure thoughts about Luke. Still, she wanted her brother to believe in her, not belittle her judgment.

"I'm sorry he's not supportive," Luke said, placing a hand on her shoulder. "If you need to talk or just vent, feel free to rant and rave around me anytime."

Kate sniffed. "Good. You're practicing what I told you about Brittany."

"What?"

"About listening and being available for her."

"Believe me, Kate, I'm not feeling anything like what I feel for my daughter."

"Oh, of course not! I didn't mean to imply you felt as strongly about me as your daughter. I know you love her and she's very important to you."

"Well, that's true, but that's not what I meant, either." He placed both hands now on her shoulders and turned her to face him more fully. "Again, I'm not doing well at explaining myself." His lips parted as if he were about to clarify, then he closed his mouth. She frowned up into his face, and finally he said, "I meant that I'm thinking of you as a man does for an attractive woman, not as a father would for a daughter."

Chapter Nine

She blinked, stunned by his words and the sincere way he'd said them. "You think I'm attractive?"

He smiled and she immediately regretted her impulsive remark. Leave it to her to jump on the one comment he'd thrown out, which probably didn't mean anything, anyway.

"Do you doubt it?"

Of course she doubted her appeal. She hadn't kept her husband's interest. She didn't exactly have men tripping over one another to ask her out. "I...I don't know. It's not something I dwell on."

"Really? Why not?"

She frowned. "Well, because I'm not that kind of person."

"What kind?"

"One who worries about how she looks all the time!"

"That's not what I said. I told you I think you're attractive, not that you're self-absorbed or vain."

She frowned again. "What's the difference?"

"Not all attractive women spend their time thinking about how attractive they are. They just know."

"I don't understand, I suppose, the nuances of self-possession."

"Can't you just believe me? I'm a pretty good judge of women, and believe me, you're attractive."

"I'm older than you are," she blurted it, then felt like slapping her hand over her mouth. Why in the world had she said that?

Luke chuckled. "That doesn't have a thing to do with how attractive you are. Or how desirable I find you."

"You find me desirable?"

He chuckled again. "Now I have to convince you of that, too?"

She shook her head. "No, I'm sorry. Forget it."

"I wish I could," he said softly, lowering his head. "Believe me, life would be a lot simpler if I could."

And then he kissed her....

LUKE KNEW HE WAS IN way over his head the moment his lips touched Kate's. She was a good girl, the kind he'd never dated, never really desired. And yet he couldn't resist the pull of her unconscious appeal. She didn't know she was beautiful, but he did.

At the last minute he stopped himself from kissing her as deeply, as intimately, as he'd like. He gentled her with his lips, coaxing a sigh and a slight melting after her initial surprise. She felt warm and soft and willing as her arms crept around his neck, and he held her without any pressure. He wanted to pull her tight against him and prove how much she affected him, but he didn't need to shock her more than he had already by kissing her.

He shouldn't be doing this. She wasn't his type. But she'd been so insecure about her desirability. What man wouldn't find her attractive?

Without giving in to the urge to use his hands and tongue and whatever other part of his anatomy he could use to bring them both pleasure, he eased away from the kiss, nibbling a little here and there until he pulled back enough to see her flushed face, dewy lips and delicate eyelids. Slowly, she opened her eyes and gazed at him.

She didn't speak. He didn't know what to say, so he simply looked at her, knowing he'd remember the sight of Kate, flushed and dreamy, for a long, long time.

"Mommy! The donkey is fussing!"

Luke stepped back, keeping a hand on Kate's arm as she wobbled and then found her balance.

"What?" she asked shakily.

"He's making a big noise like he's mad." Eddie grabbed Kate's hand, then Luke's, and tugged them both toward the door. "Come look."

Sure enough, Gordon was standing at the fence, braying across the driveway at the newest arrival at Last Chance Ranch, a bay mustang mare. "She must be in season."

"What's that?" Eddie asked.

"Uh…" Luke hadn't thought about what he'd said. He should have. He looked to Kate for guidance.

Kate smoothed her hair back behind her ears in fluttery, nervous movements, but her voice was steady when she explained, "That means the pretty little horse is looking for a daddy horse."

Good answer, Luke thought, relieved he didn't have to come up with an explanation censored for a six-year-old.

"Do you have a daddy horse?" Eddie asked, looking up with wonder in his eyes.

"No, all my horses are either girls or they're boy horses who can't be daddies."

"Why?"

Luke felt a little like squirming under Eddie's scrutiny. "Because the vet fixed them so they would be good horses who didn't ever want to be daddies and wouldn't bother the girl horses."

"Oh," Eddie said, looking quizzically around the ranch. "But—"

"Tell us about the new mare," Kate interrupted, putting her hands on Eddie's shoulders and looking at Luke. "Where did you get her?"

Once again, Kate had saved the day. "She was adopted from one of the mustang roundups the government has periodically, but didn't work out with her owners. They didn't know what to do, since they couldn't really sell her to another family when she wasn't a riding horse. They'd thought about the rendering plant in Fort Worth."

"Oh, no! She's beautiful."

"Yes, but still pretty wild." Luke hunkered down so he was eye level with Eddie. "She can't be ridden, Eddie, just like the zebras. I'm not sure how wild she is, so don't ever go near her pasture. She could really hurt you."

"Okay. I promise." He looked around again. "When are you going to get horses that people can ride?"

Luke stood up and ruffled Eddie's hair. "That's a good question. I'm going to get some riding horses soon." He had one in mind, a stunt horse named Jack that Luke had worked with about six months ago. If Jack's owner would part with him, he'd have him shipped to Texas. He'd need a horse for Brittany, though, and maybe he should get a couple of ponies for her friends.

His ranch was starting to grow by leaps and bounds, and not exactly in the direction he'd intended. He'd wanted to provide a home for neglected or abused animals, not a ranch of riding horses and pets. However, if his daughter liked horses—and he couldn't imagine why she wouldn't—he'd get whatever would make her happy.

"Eddie, we need to go home," Kate said.

"Thanks for coming by and bringing me the texts."

"Thanks for the tour." Kate said, taking Eddie's hand. "And I suppose I'll see you tomorrow morning."

"I'm looking forward to it."

She looked away, obviously uncomfortable, reading more into his comment than he meant. "I mean,

I'm anxious to get started on changing the house and changing me."

"How are you changing?" Eddie asked.

"I need to get everything ready for Brittany."

"Because you're her daddy?"

"That's right."

Eddie frowned. "Do you want to be a daddy?"

"Yes, I do."

"You didn't get fixed like the horses so you don't like girls, did you?"

"Eddie! That's not something you should ask!"

Luke laughed. He was far, far from being "fixed." "No, I didn't."

Kate shook her head and started walking toward her compact sedan. "I'm sorry, Luke."

"No problem."

She opened the passenger door and put her tote bag inside, then went to the rear door to get Eddie in the car. Before he scooted into the booster seat, he grabbed Luke's hand and tugged.

"I think my daddy got fixed so he didn't want to be a daddy anymore," the little boy said softly. "Maybe that's why he went away."

Luke froze, not sure what to say, if anything. He looked at Kate for guidance, but she appeared as stunned as he felt. What could anyone say to a child who was so obviously hurting?

"Eddie, let's talk about this at home," Kate said, her voice shaking.

"But Luke's our friend, and he's a daddy now."

Luke didn't really understand Eddie's logic, but he seemed to need to reach out to someone other than his mother to make sense out of his father's desertion.

"Yes, but he didn't know your father, so we'd better talk about him ourselves, okay?"

Eddie looked up plaintively, as if he wanted to argue with his mother but knew he shouldn't. Maybe deep down inside, he knew there were no answers.

Lord knew, Luke could understand how Eddie felt. When Ronald Lucas Simon failed to acknowledge him, Luke had been confused and angry. He'd wanted a father just like everyone else. He'd never understood why it was so easy for some men to walk away from their responsibilities. His heart went out to Eddie. He had to be hurting even more than Luke because Eddie had a father for nearly six years before the jerk left him and Kate.

"Eddie," he said as Kate buckled him in, "maybe someday soon, when I get some riding horses, you can come over and I'll give you a lesson, if that's okay with your mother."

"I can ride my uncle Travis's horses."

"That makes you almost a real cowboy, doesn't it?"

"Yep!"

"Thank you, and I'm sorry for the questions," Kate said, closing the rear door.

"It's fine. Don't worry about it." Luke put his hands in his pockets and stepped back, giving her room. He glanced one more time at Eddie, realizing the little boy had a lot in common with him. Both had been abandoned by their fathers. Eddie was still learning to cope, whereas Luke…well, he'd learned long ago to get angry, not sad, when he felt unwanted.

"And it would be best if we keep our relationship professional," she said, walking around the car.

Ah, the kiss. "You're probably right, but I'm not sorry for what happened in there."

She took a deep, uneven breath. "It won't happen again, though," she said, slipping into the driver's seat.

Luke didn't say anything as she put her key into the ignition and turned over the engine. She looked at him for a moment as if demanding his agreement, but he didn't say anything even then. She put the car into gear and drove away, glancing back every so often in the rearview mirror.

Luke placed his hands on his hips and watched her go. She would be back tomorrow, and he wouldn't kiss her again, because getting Kate's help was more important than pursuing a doomed relationship.

But he wanted to kiss her again. That, and so much more.

As EDDIE TOOK a nap, Kate tried to calm her nerves with a cup of chamomile tea and a long talk with herself about keeping her life simple. Responding to Luke's kiss had been insanity, pure and simple. If she could have done something any more stupid, any more guaranteed to mess up their relationship, she wasn't sure what it could be.

He shouldn't have kissed her in the first place, though. If he was concerned about keeping their relationship professional, he wouldn't have confessed that he found her attractive. Desirable, even. And he definitely wouldn't have stepped close enough for her to see deep into his dark eyes and recognize the loneliness they shared. He wouldn't have revealed his own vulnerability while exposing hers.

But he'd done all that and more, and like Pandora, she wasn't sure how to stuff everything back into the box.

Or even if she wanted to...

She had to, she thought as she jumped up and paced the living room. Luke was paying her well for two weeks' worth of *work*. Not pleasure. Above all, she had to keep that in mind.

She placed her tepid cup of ineffective tea on the kitchen counter. She and Eddie were due at Travis and Jodie's for dinner in about half an hour. She wasn't looking forward to another grilling by her brother, especially when she had something to feel guilty about now. That kiss. These feelings.

She didn't need this complication, and she was half-angry at Luke for putting her in this situation. The other half of the anger was directed right at herself for not pushing him away, or even saying one word to stop him. She'd even encouraged him, not that he'd taken advantage of her lapse in judgment.

She stopped abruptly just outside the kitchen. Why hadn't he taken advantage of her? Why hadn't he deepened the kiss? Because Eddie was just out-side the door, or was there another reason? Maybe he hadn't been that interested in her. Maybe he was just trying to be nice, in a strange sort of way.

Maybe he felt sorry for her.

"No," she whispered out loud. Her insecurities were showing, making her think such nonsense. Luke didn't have another agenda, he wasn't plotting some grand scheme and he had more important is-sues to worry about than boosting the ego of a di-vorced mother.

That's what she had to tell herself whenever she started slipping into such crazy thoughts, she re-minded herself. She was there to help him get ready for Brittany. Kate knew she wasn't a love interest to Luke Simon; she wasn't a sexual object to any man. She was a divorced mother, a substitute teacher, a sis-ter and a friend.

That's all, for now. Maybe later, when her life was settled, when she and Eddie had a home of their own and felt more integrated into the community of Ranger Springs. When she felt more secure, with a contracted job as a teacher. Then she could think about dating again. Not that she'd date Luke. He was too much of everything for her. Too sexy. Too intense. Too…male.

She paused at the doorway to Eddie's small bed-room. He was sprawled on the single bed, his shorts bunched up and his T-shirt rumpled like he'd been rolling around for hours. He never wanted to take a nap, but he always needed one. As long as he slept during the day, he was still her little boy. She knew before long he'd be older and would become taller and stronger so quickly.

Her little boy would be grown and she'd be… what? Still a single mother, or would she find someone else? She wasn't too old to have other children if she got busy with it soon, but she didn't see that happening. Not while she couldn't imagine dating, or spent all her free time in angst over a simple kiss rather than using that time wisely.

Still asleep, Eddie rolled to his side. If he didn't wake in a few minutes, she'd get him up so he could change for Sunday dinner. She'd put on her own best face and try to talk to her brother without getting upset or making him any more anxious than he already was. If she were really lucky, he'd admit he was wrong and apologize for his earlier remarks.

In her dreams. With a sigh, she turned away from Eddie's bedroom and went into the bathroom. She needed to freshen up before dinner. She hoped Jodie wasn't serving crow, because Kate might have to eat some after proving Travis right this afternoon.

AFTER A DINNER of roasted chicken with rice and spring vegetables, Kate couldn't eat a bite of the chocolate cake Jodie served. While Eddie devoured his piece, Travis surprised Kate by asking her to walk out to the patio.

"I'm sorry about coming on too strong earlier today," he surprised her by saying as she leaned against the rail and hugged her arms against the chill night air. "I'm just worried about you, that's all, and I have a hard time remembering that you're a grown woman."

Kate was so stunned she couldn't speak for a moment. "I'll accept your apology, big brother, but I'm a little floored. Since when do you admit you're wrong?"

"Hey, I can admit I made a slight error in judgment," he said with a sheepish grin. "I've had quite a bit of practice since I married Jodie."

"Calls you to task, does she?" Kate asked with a smile.

"At times." He sobered. "Seriously, Kate, you don't need me to tell you what to think or who to see. If you believe Luke is okay, I'll lay off the criticism."

"He's not perfect, Travis, but who is? And believe it or not, he's good with Eddie. I think we could be friends."

"Friends? Nothing more?"

She shook her head. "He's hardly my style, is he?"

"What do you mean by that?"

She shrugged. "Just that he's a young, sexy, single guy. True, he has a daughter, but that doesn't change how I see him. Riding into town on that Harley, looking like a cowboy when he strolled out of his house, acting like a white knight when he swooped Eddie up and took him to the medical clinic. That's not the kind of man…well, that I might be interested in romantically."

"You're a wonderful, beautiful woman, Kate. Any man would be lucky to have you."

Wow, two men in the same day singing her praises. "I'm not in the same league as Luke Simon and we both know it."

Travis narrowed his eyes. "Which 'we' would that be, and how do 'we' know it?"

"Oh, never mind. Just believe me when I say that my relationship with him is professional as I help him with the house, and hopefully, since we're neighbors, we can be friendly after Brittany arrives. She's going to need some friends here in Ranger Springs, poor little girl."

"Okay, I won't worry about you...for now. I don't know much about Simon, but I'm going to trust your judgment and take Hank's word."

"Thanks, Travis. I know that's hard for you."

"I love you."

Kate sighed. "I know you do, and I love you, too."

Her brother gave her a big hug. "Just keep your eyes open, okay?"

"I promise." She'd keep her eyes on her goal—making Luke into a daddy—and off his sexy good looks. And she absolutely wouldn't think about that kiss, because it wasn't going to happen again.

Chapter Ten

After Kate dropped Eddie off at school, she stopped by the Kash n' Karry for a cup of coffee and a muffin, then headed to Luke's property. The ranch road was a bit uneven and narrow, but she knew she was using the poor pavement as an excuse to drive slowly. This would be the first time she and Luke would be alone, and she was a bit apprehensive about their working relationship.

For one thing, how was she going to make him into a good father when she knew so little about him? Whether he'd been around children, such as nieces or nephews, or the children of friends. Or if he knew absolutely nothing about kids, even though he was good with Eddie. Very good, except when faced with some hard questions as any six-year-old would sometimes ask.

At least Brittany wasn't a baby. He didn't need to know how to change diapers or make up bottles of formula. She was probably a fairly self-reliant child if her uncle was a truck driver and her mother was gone. Even before her mother's death, Brittany had probably helped out in the kitchen or around the house. Kate knew that was true with most children of working mothers.

So she supposed she'd concentrate on parenting skills such as listening, discipline, school, friends and family relations. She rather disliked holding herself up as an expert on any of those subjects, with the possible exception of school, but Luke seemed to believe she could impart some knowledge, so she'd do her best. At least the information was fresh in her mind from studying so recently to get back into the classroom.

Her car bumped over the cattle guard at the entrance to Luke's property. She always wondered why cattle didn't figure out they could jump over the metal bars placed across a ditch. Or maybe cattle couldn't jump. She was as ignorant of livestock as Luke claimed to be of little girls.

As she pulled up to the gravel area between the house and barn, she noticed two trucks belonging to workers, with their Branson Construction company logos on the doors. The sound of power tools and the odor of paint wafted out from inside. Luke was nowhere in sight, so she got out with her tote bag and coffee, locked the car and headed toward the barn. She had an idea he might be there, escaping from the noise and smells of home renovation.

She found him in the wide area between the stalls,

working with one of the ponies she'd seen in the pasture. "I thought none of your animals performed any longer, except at schools when you're trying to be especially nice," she said as she set her bag on what looked like clean hay.

Luke raised his eyebrows in surprise, then gave her a quick perusal. If he'd lingered a little longer, she would have considered the look sexual. But he quickly turned his attention back to the pony. "They don't usually, but I got a call from a wrangler friend who's working on a movie. They want to spoof that famous Clydesdale commercial where the horses are playing football. He thought I might be able to help, and sure enough, both Spot and Potsy are trained to place their forelegs on a stand."

"How will that look like football?"

"They'll shoot in front of a green screen, take out the stand and put in a soccer ball. Then they'll animate another pony's foreleg to make it look like he's kicking the ball."

"Sounds very high-tech."

"So much can be done with computers now that real animals sometimes aren't even used. However, they want this to look as much like the original as possible, and real horses were used for that commercial."

"I know you have some obligations to get the ponies ready, but we also have to work on getting you ready for your daughter."

"I won't be long. Just have a seat over there," he

said, pointing to a stack of hay bales, "and I'll be done as soon as I get them accustomed to this stand."

With a sigh, Kate sat on the bales and sipped her rapidly cooling coffee. Luke worked patiently with first one pony, then the other, letting them circle the round, green metal object and sniff it. Then Luke stepped onto the stand, as if explaining to the ponies that it was safe. When both animals seemed comfortable with the new item, he gave them each a piece of apple and led them outside to the pasture.

"We can get started now," he said, walking quickly back into the barn. "I wasn't sure what time you were coming over, so I was trying to get in a little training early. At their age I don't want to wear them out."

"I understand. You're very patient, by the way. That's a great trait for parents." She smiled, thinking about how trying any child could be. "Even if Brittany is a great child, you'll need patience. Just don't rush her into accepting anything in her new life, except simple rules for her safety, of course." That's something Eddie had a big problem with, so Kate maybe wasn't the best source on how to keep a child on the straight and narrow.

"I'll do my best to give her time," Luke said. "There's so much to learn, to think about."

"I know, but you're really good with Eddie. I noticed that when we were at dinner and also yesterday. You'll be fine with Brittany."

"Thanks," he said, looking away.

He seemed a little uncomfortable with praise, so she

changed the subject. "I'm concerned about where we'll be working. The house appears to be…occupied."

"Yeah, they're making a mess in there," he said, putting his hands on his hips and gazing out the barn door. "They'll be finished by the weekend, but that doesn't help us today."

"It's not too hot yet. We can work out here if you'd like," she offered.

"Are you sure? This isn't what you're used to."

"A little dust and hay won't bother me."

"But your clothes and your shoes will be a mess."

"They'll clean up."

He looked at her as if he didn't believe her.

"What?"

"I don't think of you as someone who would spend time around horses and barns and dust, except maybe at a polo match or a fancy racetrack."

Kate laughed. "I don't go to polo matches, and the only racetrack I've been to was with a group of friends for a birthday, and believe me, I didn't know anything about horses or betting. I'm a city girl, but I'm learning to like the country."

"Still, I don't want to offend you."

"Don't be silly! I'm enjoying the fresh air."

He paused for a moment, then said, "You're very gracious."

"Why, that's a wonderful compliment. Thank you."

Luke narrowed his eyes and tilted his head slightly. "You're doing that schoolteacher thing again, aren't you?"

"What do you mean?"

"You're trying to put me in my place by getting all businesslike."

"I thought we did have a professional relationship. Was I wrong?" She held her breath as she waited for him to argue with her.

He looked at her until she felt like squirming, then shook his head. "No, we're all professional here." Was he thinking of the kiss? Regretting it? She had no idea because he was difficult to read. Or maybe she simply didn't know much about men. She'd misread—or failed to read—her husband countless times.

Luke dusted his hands off on the rear of his jeans. "So, where do we start?"

BECAUSE THE HOUSE was a mess, Luke reluctantly suggested they go into town for lunch. He wasn't looking forward to the stares of the locals, but he didn't see any options. Maybe Kate would choose the fast-food place.

"Lunch? I'm starving," she said as she placed a book inside her ever-present tote bag. "Is the Four Square Café okay? Monday is chicken and dumplings day."

"Sure. Let's go."

Luke drove. With the windows down, the warm wind whipped around them. Kate produced something to put her hair into a ponytail—he'd have to get some of those for Brittany—and added sunglasses against the noontime glare. She looked happy and relaxed, which was surprising, considering the way they'd spent the last few minutes before parting yesterday. He'd assumed she would be more tense around him while they were truly alone. At least at the ranch, there had been workers in the house, coming and going from the trucks.

Maybe Kate wasn't as fragile as he'd originally thought.

Just as they entered the "downtown" area of Ranger Springs, Kate said, "Look, there's Dr. Wheatley and his wife." Kate waved as they passed a blue sedan paused at a stop sign on a side street.

Great. Joyce Wheatley was one of the biggest gossips in town, along with her cohort, Thelma Rogers, another regular at the café. Both ladies seemed nice, but boy, did they know what was going on in Ranger Springs. Everyone would be talking about Kate driving around with him. He only hoped he didn't hurt her reputation. She was, after all, an upstanding elementary schoolteacher.

But he needed her help, and he didn't feel guilty about asking her to educate him on eight-year-old girls.

"I suppose we should stop by the Robin's Nest and talk to Robin Parker," she said as they started around the square. "She'll be very helpful for decorating Brittany's room, and probably with the other renovations, unless you have something already planned."

"No, I've been more concerned about the place being structurally sound and functional. I know the decorating stuff is important, though, especially to women. Females, I should say, since Brittany is just a little girl."

"Yes, she's a girl, but make sure you don't refer to her as 'just a little girl' in her presence. Children that age think they are far more mature than they really are. They don't appreciate adults bursting their bubbles."

"I'll try to remember that."

"But don't expect her to act older than her years, even though she's been through a lot. She'll want to lean on you, depend on you, although she won't want her need for assurance and stability to be obvious."

"Fatherhood is getting more and more complicated," he observed as he pulled the truck to a stop in a parking spot between the café and the corner next to Schuler's Jewelry.

Kate chuckled. "Wait until she actually arrives."

THAT EVENING, after Eddie was tucked into bed and the dishes were washed, Kate relaxed on the couch and took inventory of the day. She'd made progress with Luke, mainly by bringing up topics as they naturally occurred. She'd originally planned to be more structured, but that didn't seem to work with a man who had chores to do and a renovation to oversee.

Besides making progress on turning Luke into a dad, she was most proud of her ability to be professional. Several times she'd had to force herself not to stare, to touch or otherwise humiliate herself with Luke. More than once she'd glanced at his mouth and remembered their kiss. But every time, she'd controlled her wild impulses to make a fool of herself with a man who obviously couldn't be interested in her despite his flattering words the other day.

And that's all they were, she convinced herself. He probably flattered all women, just out of habit. She wasn't going to take it personally.

He'd had no trouble staying focused today, either, so things were working out fine. They were each doing what they were supposed to do.

She picked up a pillow and hugged it to that empty spot directly below her heart. If everything was so great, why did she feel so…deflated? Did she really think that Luke would admit he'd meant everything he said the day before, that he couldn't live another minute without kissing her again? No, of course not. That was just plain silly.

If either one of them gave in to such crazy urges, they'd never accomplish their individual goals. Luke wouldn't be prepared for Brittany and Kate wouldn't have enough money to get a place of her own this fall.

She would do the right thing and earn every penny Luke was paying her. She'd help him with the house and anything else for the next two weeks. She'd feel a sense of accomplishment when Brittany arrived and was welcomed into her new family, her new home.

None of that would happen if she and Luke got personal, and that was unacceptable.

THE NEXT DAY started much as the first day on the job. Kate arrived after Eddie went to school. The workers were already hammering, sawing and painting inside the house. Luke was in the barn, working with the ponies. Kate stood in the doorway and watched him, trying very hard not to admire the play of muscles beneath the white T-shirt or long to smooth back his dark, thick hair as it waved over his forehead. With a sigh, she sat on a bale of hay and waited for him to finish.

In a few minutes, he led the ponies toward their pasture and placed the metal stand in front of a stall, next to a pile of fresh hay and a bucket. "Would you like to see something cute?" he asked, finally acknowledging her.

"Sure." She stood and brushed the rear of her jeans.

He crooked his finger and smiled, and it was all she could do not to run toward him with a silly grin.

"Step up here," he said, nodding toward the stand the ponies had just used.

"Are you training me now?" she asked jokingly.

"That's not my job," he said, smiling in reply. "You're the teacher."

I'll bet you could teach me quite a few things I never learned in books...or anywhere else, she thought, shocking herself at the way her mind kept coming back to intimate speculation about Luke. She stepped onto the metal stand and peered into the stall.

A tiny pony and her even smaller foal stood near the back wall. "Oh, they're darling."

"They arrived last night from a ranch outside

Blanco. The county agent picked them up. Their owner moved away and the stock was abandoned."

"Oh, is she okay? The mare had a tangled tail and her coat wasn't sleek, but she didn't look sick or injured.

"She's underweight and was a little dehydrated, but nothing too serious or she'd be at a vet clinic instead."

"Will you keep her?"

"Probably. They don't know who to contact because the place was being rented and the guy skipped out."

"Brittany will love her."

"Do you think so?"

"How could she not? They're both precious."

"That's a good name."

"Oh, no, I didn't mean to name her."

"I want you to name the mare. I'll ask Brittany to name the foal."

"That's…thank you."

"Precious is a good name for a miniature horse."

"She's not a pony?"

"The breed is called a miniature horse, even though they look like small ponies."

"Oh." Kate took another look at the mare, nudging the cuddly foal toward her flank to nurse, then sighed and turned back to look at Luke, who stood beside her at the wooden planks of the stall. Because of the metal stand, she stood eye to eye with him. Close enough she could see mischief brewing in his dark eyes and feel overwhelmed by his masculine scent.

"We should probably get to work," she whispered.

"You're right." His breath smelled like mint and

his lips looked soft yet firm, especially when he smiled ever so slightly.

Kate blinked and leaned back. "Okay, then!" she said briskly, searching deep inside for professionalism. *He doesn't mean to be so sexy,* she told herself. *That's just the way he is.*

"Kate?"

"Let's get started." Without waiting for him to help her down from the stand, she took a step.

"Let me—" he started to say, moving his arm to encircle her waist and then her foot slipped on the uneven floor by the stall. She lost her balance, and when she tried to right herself, her momentum sent him backward. Before she knew what was happening, he tripped and brought her down with him.

They landed in a pile of hay, Luke on his back, her straddling his legs.

"I'm so sorry," she wheezed, dust from the hay rising around them. "Are you okay?"

Luke started to laugh. "I'm fine."

She finally realized that his other hand was at her waist and she was in what could only be called a compromising position. "I'm sorry," she said again, leaning forward to get her hand on the floor so she could push herself up, bringing her even closer to Luke. But she couldn't help it; she needed to get up now, so she didn't do something else really stupid.

Before she could lever herself off the floor—and him—Luke's hands crept up her back and tugged her down. She landed flat against his stomach and chest. "I'm not complaining," he said softly with those firm, soft lips, with that minty breath. And then he pulled her even closer, one hand on the back of her head, and she closed her eyes as he kissed her.

This time the kiss wasn't tentative or sweet. It was commanding and powerful, and she just about melted all over his denim and cotton. Her arms snaked around his neck and her fingers slid through his hair. Her heart beat fast and hard as she molded herself as tightly as possible to him. The kiss went on and on, until Luke moaned and pressed upward where he really shouldn't be pressing, but it felt so good.

She broke the kiss, breathless and wild and not really knowing why she was lying on the floor of a barn with Luke Simon.

"Maybe we should get up now," she said, her voice soft and not at all professional.

"Are you sure?" he asked, his voice deep and slightly breathless and oh so sexy.

Chapter Eleven

Luke pulled Kate up from the barn floor, knowing he shouldn't say anything about all the hay stuck to her plaid shirt and jeans. Or the dusty smudges on her clothes. His handprints, no doubt. He hadn't been able to stop himself from holding her, pulling her close and kissing her.

Crazy. He was a madman, pure and simple. What was he thinking? Nothing. That was the problem. He hadn't been thinking at all, at least not with his brain.

"That wasn't part of the lesson plan," she said shakily, dusting off her calves and thighs and hips.

"I know." He sighed and looked away before he offered to help her. He wasn't sure how much dust and hay he'd remove, but the effort would be…rewarding. "I don't seem to have as much self-control as I like to believe I possess. You…you tie me up in knots."

"I…what?"

He looked away from Kate's beautiful, refined

features. Even with her hair in disarray and dust on her clothing, she looked like a lady.

A lady he'd dragged down into the hay.

"You're not like any other woman I've known, Kate. I shouldn't have kissed you. I don't have the right."

"Because we're working together," she stated flatly.

He turned back around. "No, because we're two different types of people. I'm...well, let's just say that I'm your opposite."

"Luke, it's true we're at different places in our lives but—"

"Oh, you're different all right. I never, and I mean never, date women who don't know the score. The women I spend time with just want to have fun. They know I'm not getting serious. They know I'm not going to ask them to stay. I might not remember their name in a month or two."

"That sounds like a lonely way to live," she said softly.

"It's my life, Kate. You have 'serious' written all over you. You're a staying kind of woman."

"My ex-husband didn't think so." She withdrew her hand from his arm and leaned against the stall. "He just kept several fun-loving women to spend time with." Kate laughed without any humor. "Silly me, I just thought he was devoted to his job, his clients."

"That doesn't have anything to do with you, Kate. His behavior was all about him."

"How can you know that? You don't know Ed."

"I'm a man, so believe me, I know."

She shook her head. "You're just trying to make me feel better, but—"

"I'm not trying to make you feel better! I'm trying to make you see the truth. You're a beautiful, desirable woman and I'm not the kind of man who should be kissing you."

"You are a fine man, Luke Simon. A good man. Er, not that you should be kissing me. But there's a sweetness about you that you try to hide."

"I am not sweet!"

She laughed. "Yes, you are."

He frowned. "I grew up without a permanent home, with a single mother and no father." He didn't tell Kate any more about the man who'd fathered him, about that nonrelationship and the other family Luke would never know.

"Luke, your lack of a father isn't important. Your mother was obviously an exceptional woman."

"What makes you say that?"

"Because she raised you to be a sweet, good, caring man."

He threw up his hands. "I give up. If you say I'm sweet, then how can I argue?"

"Exactly. Never argue with a strong-willed woman."

"I'll try to remember that."

They stood inside the barn, looking at each other, not touching, as different as night and day despite Kate's insistence that they weren't. As for keeping their relationship purely business…well, that wasn't a success.

"We'd better get to work," she said finally.

"You're right. The clock is ticking." Brittany would be here whether he and Kate agreed, whether they kissed again…or not. He might not be a great candidate for a friend or a lover, but he would learn how to be a dad if it took every minute of the next week and a half. If it took every cent he'd earned in Hollywood. If it took all his concentration to stay on topic and away from Kate.

BY THE END of the week, Robin Parker had been out to the ranch and collaborated with Luke on a design plan for Brittany's room. She'd also made suggestions about the final paint colors for the living room, dining room and study. Luke liked her ideas so much that he decided to paint everything a buttery gold instead of the stark white he'd originally planned. Kate thought that showed he was flexible and easygoing, but she didn't tell him that because he'd probably argue with her.

He didn't see himself as noble or sensitive or affectionate. What did he think having all these misfit animals meant? He cared enough to see to their health and happiness. He also cared enough to make sure his daughter was welcomed warmly, in a cozy home with a room decorated just for her.

This Saturday morning, Travis was watching Eddie, and Kate was going with Luke to shop for furniture in nearby San Marcus. If they didn't find what they needed there, they might have to drive to Austin or San Antonio.

"Are you sure you don't mind keeping Eddie today?" Kate asked her brother as she stood just inside his kitchen.

"Not at all. With Jodie away on that photo shoot for her new line of perfume, I'm home with Marsha anyway. Eddie can help me keep her entertained. Besides," Travis said, winking at Eddie, "we guys have to stick together. We're way outnumbered by women in this family."

"You'll have to talk to Jodie about that," Kate said, shaking her head. "A little brother for Marsha would be nice."

"She's thinking about it. I told her I'd be willing to cooperate at any time."

"Too much information, big brother," Kate said, holding up her hand. She heard a truck pull up in the drive and looked out the window. "My ride's here," she said, purposefully avoiding Luke's name so she didn't set Travis off again. Although, she had to admit, he'd been less critical of both their neighbor and her judgment lately.

"I'll be back as soon as possible."

"Don't worry about it. Eddie and I will be fine."

"Okay." She leaned down and kissed her son on the cheek, smiling when he wiped away her lip gloss. "Be good for Uncle Travis."

"Bring me something?"

"I'll try. Mostly, we're going to furniture stores."

"Yeah, for Brittany," Eddie said, disappointed.

"What's wrong?"

"When am I going to meet her? All I hear is Brittany, Brittany, Brittany."

Kate laughed. "Very soon. She'll be here when her spring break comes, remember? We'll make her feel welcome."

"I guess."

Kate figured Eddie was slightly jealous of the little girl who consumed so much of Luke's time and attention.

"You have your cell phone?" Travis asked.

"I sure do. I'll see you both soon."

"Bye, Mommy."

She kissed Eddie's cheek again, then waved at Travis before hurrying out the door. She didn't want to keep Luke waiting. She wasn't rushing, she told herself, because she was looking forward to seeing him. They'd maintained a professional relationship after that kiss in the hay on Tuesday. Thank goodness. She didn't have the will or the methods to thwart Luke if he'd wanted to kiss her again.

He stood outside the truck by the passenger door, looking casual yet polished in new jeans and a Western shirt with colorful wide stripes. He had to have taken his clothes to the laundry in town because they were nicely starched.

"You look spiffy," she said, hoisting herself up onto the passenger seat as Luke held the door.

"Thanks. You look good, too."

She'd worn a khaki skirt for a change from her jeans, since they weren't going to be at the ranch all day. She wasn't sure how long they'd be gone. Luke needed almost everything, from linens to furniture.

Once they were on the state highway, she asked, "Did you ship anything from California that still has to be unpacked?"

"No, pretty much everything I own is already in the house. When I get the rest of the furniture I need, maybe you can help me put it in place."

"Sure. You don't have many personal things, do you?"

"No, I never did collect stuff like photos and furniture. I wasn't sure where I'd be staying next month, so it seemed silly to hang on to it. My mother wasn't one to collect things, either, and I guess I take after her."

Kate suspected that his lack of personal possessions had more to do with his inability to put down roots than it did with DNA from his mother. She'd already commented to him that he needed to integrate more into the community, which he seemed to find difficult. He'd said he hadn't had a relationship with his father, so maybe that gap in Luke's childhood still affected him. She didn't want to overanalyze Luke, but she couldn't help thinking about his past. "Did she move a lot also?" Kate asked.

"Yeah, we moved fairly often," he said in a voice that told her he wasn't going to discuss himself much further.

"You know, little girls tend to collect things and keep them forever. Or at least until they go away to college."

"I want Brittany to have whatever she wants… within reason, naturally. And I definitely want her to go to college. I suppose I should start one of those college funds for her."

"Perhaps. You'll need a lawyer and maybe a financial planner, too, because you'll want to make sure she's provided for in your will in case something happens to you."

"Damn, I hadn't thought of that yet. Sometimes I feel completely at a loss. What if I don't think of everything?"

"Luke, anyone can hire a decorator or buy clothes or furniture for a little girl, but not everyone can supply love and support. You're her *father.* That means so much."

He was silent for a moment, then said, "I'm just glad that you're helping me. I'm really out of my element here."

"That's understandable. I'd be out of mine if I had to train horses or even care for your animals."

"Yeah, well, my work isn't all that complicated, whereas you're in charge of teaching kids how to read and do math and all those other things they'll need to know. I wouldn't have a clue where to start."

"Please, don't remind me. I feel overwhelmed enough."

"You do?" He glanced at her, his expression showing surprise, before turning his attention back to the road.

"Of course. I've never really taught, or I should

say, been completely in charge of a classroom. I did my student teaching, graduated from college, then settled into married life. I had Eddie and assumed I might teach in the future. Not support myself. Not be a single mom. This wasn't part of my plans, and quite frankly—and please don't tell anyone on the school board or in the administration—I'm a little worried about pulling it all together."

"You never seem worried. You're always so calm, except when Eddie fell off the zebra, but that doesn't count because it was an emergency."

"I was glad you were there. You were the calm one. Sometimes, though, I'm not so sure of myself as I might seem to others. Sometimes I sit alone in the apartment and wonder how Eddie is going to survive his mother's nervous breakdown. Other times, I feel pretty good about the future."

Luke fell silent for a while, then said, "I guess we all go through that. Ever since I discovered Brittany, I've been the same way."

"You're going to be fine. Do you know when the agency is going to do a home visit?"

"No, but I hope they'll be here by the end of next week. If not, Brittany is moving in anyway. I'd just like to get everything straightened out legally."

"Is her birth certificate changed?"

"It's in the works. I've submitted everything to the Florida officials. Her airline ticket is purchased—one way from Orlando to San Antonio."

"That's good. That makes it seem much more real, doesn't it?"

"Yeah, it does, and it's kind of scary."

"Just keep her safe, well fed and happy. The rest will fall into place."

"Lord, I hope so. I feel like the most ill-prepared father in history."

Kate laughed, even though she didn't feel so amused. "No, I believe Ed Wooten was the most ill-prepared father in history. And, unlike you, he had no interest in improving. Unfortunately for Eddie, and for me, I didn't see that until after he was already born."

"Do you regret having a child?"

"Never," she said immediately. "Eddie is wonderful, and you're going to feel much more relaxed as soon as Brittany moves in." She hoped Luke believed her.

THEY STOPPED for an early dinner on the way home after checking with Travis to make sure Eddie was okay. Luke encouraged Kate to order a margarita or whatever she'd like, since he was driving and drinking iced tea. She remarked about getting out so seldom, then ordered a chardonnay. Kate was a good mother, an intelligent woman and deserved to go on more dates. Not that *they* were dating. He was simply treating her to a meal after a successful shopping trip, enjoying her company before they each returned home.

She'd get herself back together soon. She'd start that teaching job she mentioned, get her own place and then find herself another husband. Someone to give Eddie a little brother or sister.

The idea of Kate with another man left a bitter taste in Luke's mouth that not even a gallon of sweet tea could eliminate.

Once their food arrived, they commented mostly on the meal and stopped talking about anything personal. That was fine with him. He needed a little space to remind him that Kate wasn't the kind of woman he dated. She wasn't loose or flamboyant. She didn't sleep around. She wasn't casual about anything, especially sex.

After he paid the check and they walked out to the late-afternoon sunshine, Kate squinted against the bright light. The unpaved parking lot was uneven and on a hill, and after only one glass of wine, Kate seemed a little intoxicated. He offered his arm and she took it.

She actually giggled as she clung to him. "I don't ever remember being this silly after one glass of wine," she said as they walked side by side up the hill.

He didn't mention that it had been a very large wineglass. "You deserve to be a little silly once in a while."

As they neared the truck, she tripped on a root and toppled against him. He grabbed her shoulders and steadied her as she laughed up at his startled expression. She looked so young and happy and carefree that he smiled backed, then grinned. "You're tipsy."

"I know. And you're cute."

Surprised, he chuckled at her comment, but then

she reached up and touched his cheek—that dimple that was about the only feature he shared with his father—and all his good intentions evaporated. His smile faded as her eyes got that come-hither look and he captured her finger in his hand. Bringing it to his lips, he kissed the tip, then sucked the end into his mouth.

"Umm, dessert," he murmured.

"I think I'm *too* tipsy for this," she whispered.

"I haven't had a thing to drink, but I don't think I can sober up in time."

"In time for what?"

"In time to stop myself from doing this." He leaned down and captured her parted lips in his, kissing her deeply as he pulled her body against his. She molded herself tightly to him, then wrapped her arms around his neck and kissed him back.

"Luke," she whispered when he came up for air.

"I'm right here," he said, nibbling beside her mouth.

"This feels so good that it must be wrong."

Chapter Twelve

This was wrong. She was so right. They were supposed to be resisting these urges to kiss, and instead
he'd jumped right into the feelings.

He stopped kissing her and leaned his forehead
against hers. "I'm sorry. You're right. You'd think I
was the one who'd had wine instead of iced tea. All
I can say is that you make me tipsy."

"Oh, that's so sweet."

"There you go again, calling me sweet. As I see
things, I'm the guy who's trying to seduce you in a
restaurant parking lot in broad daylight."

"You're trying to seduce me?"

"Oh, never mind. You don't have a bit of self-
preservation. I have to be strong for both of us."

"I think that would be a very good idea," she agreed.

He took her arm and steered her toward the truck.
"We're going back home—our individual homes—
before I do something very unprofessional."

"Another good idea," she said, suddenly sounding

much more sober. "As soon as we get back to real-ity, this attraction thing will go away."

"Right." He helped her into the passenger side and thought to himself, wrong. Wrong, wrong, wrong. That's what his desire for Kate was. This crazy attraction wasn't going away. He'd just have to control it, because they had one more week before he had to be ready for Brittany.

He didn't have time to get involved with any woman…and especially not someone like Kate, whom he couldn't walk away from after a couple of nights. Kate didn't have any experience with mean-ingless flings. He wasn't going to enlighten her on how to love 'em and leave 'em.

BY THE TIME Luke pulled into the driveway by her ga-rage apartment, Kate's headache had begun and her mortification was complete. She'd made a complete fool of herself in the parking lot of the restaurant. Right in public! What had she been thinking?

Nothing. That was the problem. She'd only been feeling, letting her emotions get the better of her due to one glass of wine. One! She couldn't really blame it all on the alcohol. She had a deep and abiding weakness where Luke Simon was concerned.

She had ever since he'd ridden into town that day. She'd never been attracted to tall, dark and danger-ous men. Maybe she should have dated a few before she married the seemingly perfect man. Maybe she was spreading her wings after years of a bland marriage. Perhaps Ed's disinterest in her, his disrespect for their marriage, had made her see life—and men— differently. Maybe.

"Are you okay?" Luke asked as he turned off the engine.

She nodded as she sat there in the early evening, with the sunlight filtering through the hackberry and cottonwood trees and fluttering around the dashboard of the truck like demented moths. "I'm fine. I'll just go get Eddie and...I have lots to do."

"Will I see you tomorrow?"

She looked up at Luke. "Of course."

"I wasn't sure. You've been awfully quiet after..."

"I'm sorry about that." She shook her head. "I don't know why I keep...well, acting inappropriately. You must think I'm some kind of desperate divorcée who throws herself at men."

"You didn't throw yourself at me. You just flirted a little. Let's blame it on the wine and try to forget it."

"Do you think we can?"

"I definitely think we should."

"Okay, then." If he could, so could she. She hoped.

He smoothed a strand of hair back from her cheek. "Maybe you should get a good night's sleep, take a day off tomorrow and we'll begin over again on Monday."

His touch felt so good, so right. She wanted to lean into his hand and stay there forever. She jerked upright. No, she didn't. She wanted to be independent, to start her life over with a new career. "Yes. That sounds good. Everything will be back to normal Monday."

"Right," he said as he reached for the steering wheel.

"Okay, then. Thanks for the dinner. I think Brittany will love the furniture, and I'll see you on Monday."

Luke nodded and sat there, staring out the windshield and not at her as she opened the door and hurried toward her brother's house.

Travis met her at the back door, Marsha in his arms. Kate smiled at the baby and gave her loud kisses on the cheek, making Marsha giggle. Eddie had to be watching television; she heard the set on in the family room.

"That was interesting," Travis said with a frown as she slipped through the door and walked toward the family room.

"This isn't a good time to pick a fight," she said.

"I'm just curious about this *professional* relationship you claim to have with a man who makes all those emotions flash across your face."

"You shouldn't be spying on me," she replied in a low voice so Eddie wouldn't hear as she turned to confront her brother. "And you don't know what you're talking about."

"I know what I saw. Is he putting pressure on you to do anything you don't want to do?"

"Of course not! He was a perfect gentleman." She'd been the instigator.

"I just want you to be careful. You haven't dated since Ed—"

"No, and I'm not dating now." She stood a little

straighter and continued talking before Travis could say anything else. "I'm sorry I was gone so long. We had a lot of shopping to do. We had to go all the way to the north side of San Antonio to find the furniture we needed, then to the outlet mall, and by then we were both hungry."

"Gee, sounds like you two are setting up house-keeping."

She threw up her hands in desperation. "That's ridiculous. I'm taking my son home now."

Travis sighed. "Just listen. Sometimes when you look at Luke or talk about him, it's like back when you didn't know why guys wanted to get you alone in their cars."

That stopped her. "It is not!"

"Yeah, it is, and it kind of scares me."

It scares me too, Kate thought as she hurried toward her son. But like Luke had said, they'd forget about it and focus on their other relationship. The one that wasn't a minefield of painful repercussions.

ON MONDAY Luke was visited by a child-welfare official who reviewed his home, the renovation almost finished, and listened to him explain his plans for himself, his ranch and Brittany. He had to have said the right things, because the woman was smiling when she left and said she'd forward a copy of her report to the Florida court.

He breathed a sigh of relief when her sedan pulled across the cattle guard onto the road.

"How did it go?" Kate asked, coming through the front door. She watched the departing car also.

"Fine, I guess. She was friendly."

"Hmm. She probably enjoyed spending time with you."

Luke frowned. "What does that mean?"

Kate took a deep breath. "Never mind."

"You're jealous!"

"I most certainly am not!" She turned and went back into the house. "I simply made an observation. Now I'm going to get back to sorting these books for Brittany. As soon as the furniture gets here, we need to get it in place and add the accessories Robin picked out."

He followed her into the newly painted bedroom that Brittany would inhabit in just about a week. "Do you think we made the right choice? White furniture doesn't seem too practical for a kid."

"On the contrary, the furniture is cream, not white, and if she does get it dirty, you can see the smudges and clean them. Or have her help you clean it. Dirt doesn't show up as much on natural or stained wood, so really, it can become much more dirty."

"Okay, but what about the whole ocean theme? I was thinking something more to do with animals."

"You mean mammals, and that's your passion, not necessarily hers. Robin and I both agree that the ocean theme will make her less homesick for Florida."

"I don't even know if she likes all those fish the artist is going to paint on the walls," he said as he looked at the ocean-blue paint above a sandy-tan color at the bottom of the wall.

"She'll love the total look. There will be fish and dolphins cavorting through this ocean, and seashells and starfish and other creatures on the sandy bottom."

"Still, maybe we should have gone with the circus idea."

"Not all children like circuses. You're projecting."

"Projecting?"

"And worrying."

He frowned. "Maybe. I want the room to be perfect."

Kate placed her hands on her hips and faced him. "Tell me this. What are you going to do if she doesn't like it?"

He thought for only a moment. "Offer to change it?"

"Right. So besides the expense of hiring the mural painter and buying the bedspread and curtains, there won't be a problem."

"I suppose. But I want her to love her new room."

Kate took him by the arms and looked into his eyes, her expression serious and determined. "No, you want Brittany to love her new dad. And she will. Believe me, she will."

Kate was right. He did want his daughter to love him. He'd never wanted someone's love before. He'd always been sure of his mother's love. His father— well, he'd been just as sure of the bastard's disinterest, until it was too late. However, the uncertainty of Brittany's feelings made him wish all this was over and everything was perfect and he could get on with life, everyone happy and healthy.

"You're going to be a great father."

He wished he could be as certain as Kate.

KATE HAD FELT the tension escalate all week as the furniture was put in place, the accessories added, the kitchen put in order and the mural completed just in time.

Brittany would be here tomorrow afternoon.

Kate had left Luke's ranch to pick up Eddie from school. They went to Robin's Nest to get a welcome gift for Brittany, then stopped for fast food before going home. Even Eddie seemed excited, but tired. She hoped he'd sleep well tonight because she was exhausted.

Or maybe she wasn't so much physically exhausted as she was tense with anticipation. Despite all her efforts and assurances, Luke still had doubts. Personally, she thought he was doing great, but it was impossible to convince someone that he was competent, had excellent instincts and would succeed beyond his expectations.

As Eddie watched one of his favorite shows on television, Kate relaxed in a tub filled with warm water and vanilla-scented bubbles. With any luck, she could get to bed right after Eddie. She closed her eyes and thought about the past two weeks. Luke was such a nice man. Even when he was worried sick and faced with unfamiliar obstacles, he kept his patience. He didn't rant and rave, or get moody or surly. And despite their ill-advised kisses, he hadn't taken advantage of her weakness for him.

So, she thought as she eased deeper into the water, to recap: Luke was determined, patient, even-tempered, noble and, most of all, a fantastic kisser.

Her eyes snapped open. No, that's not what she was supposed to be thinking! She was such a confused mass of memories and emotions.

After tomorrow, when Brittany was safely here and Luke could relax, things would return to normal. She'd enjoy spring break with her son, go back to substitute teaching and only see Luke around town or if Eddie got a wild urge to visit the animals. Maybe they could arrange some play time for Brittany and Eddie, if the children got along. It was hard to say because a two-year age difference was huge when kids were six and eight.

Two years wasn't such a big age difference when the people were thirty and thirty-two. Not that she should be thinking about that, either.

The water started to cool, so she shaved her legs quickly and finished scrubbing with the exfoliating puff Jodie insisted she use daily. Her sister-in-law was a fount of information about beauty and skin care, some of which actually seemed practical, and not just for women interested in attracting men. Which Kate wasn't. At least not in the near future.

She and Eddie shared a couple of shortbread cookies and two glasses of milk before his bedtime. Dressed in her soft cotton short pajamas, she was already getting sleepy when the phone rang.

"Hello."

"Kate, it's Luke."

She heard the barely controlled panic in his voice. "What's wrong?"

"I don't know. Everything. Maybe nothing. I'm just not sure I'm ready for this."

"You're ready. You're doing great."

"That's easy for you to say. Brittany isn't going to be judging you."

"Judging? No, that's not what she's going to do."

"How can you be sure?"

Kate had a feeling this conversation was only going to get more intense. She couldn't reassure him over the phone. He was stressed out, understandably, and needed her.

But she shouldn't see him now, especially since it was night and they never saw each other except in broad daylight.

"Luke, you're going to be a great father. Remember how well you've interacted with Eddie? How I've mentioned you have great instincts?"

"That's fine, but I already know Eddie. And Brittany is a girl, someone I've mostly just talked to on the phone." Kate's heart went out to him because she knew how much he cared. She wished Eddie's father cared half as much as Luke about relating to his child.

"Kate, I'm really worried."

"I know, but—"

"Mommy, who is it?" Eddie asked, rubbing his eyes.

She asked Luke to wait a minute, put her hand over the phone and said to her son, "It's Luke, sweetie. You know how I've been helping him? Well," she said, taking a deep breath, "he needs me one more time before his daughter gets here tomorrow."

"Oh."

"I'll be with you in just a minute, Eddie." He walked off to finish his cookie and she returned to the phone. "Luke, I'm going to be over there shortly. I have to take Eddie to Travis and Jodie."

"No, Kate, it's too late for you to come out."

"Don't be silly. It's not even nine o'clock, and you obviously need to talk. I'll be right over. Leave the porch light on for me, okay."

"Okay. And Kate? Thanks."

He disconnected the call and she rushed to the bedroom. She pulled on underwear, jeans and a clean T-shirt, then went back into the kitchen. She had no idea how long Luke needed to talk and she wasn't willing to drag her son out of bed in the middle of the night if it wasn't necessary.

"Eddie, I'm going to ask Travis and Jodie if you can go to sleep at their house tonight, okay?"

"Okay. Can I sleep there all night? Uncle Travis fixes blueberry pancakes on Sunday morning."

"Yes, he does. I'll call him and make sure it's okay for you to come over."

Within a few minutes, she'd put Eddie's things together and walked him over to the main house. Jodie was back home and they were glad to have Eddie spend the night. Travis did, however, give her a look that showed his disapproval of her running off to the neighbor's.

"I'll see you in the morning," she told her brother and sister-in-law. Eddie was already upstairs, checking on baby Marsha. Kate hurried off before Travis could quiz her.

The night was clear and pleasant as she drove around to Luke's ranch. Although she could walk—or chase Eddie—through the pasture in just minutes, the drive took longer as the road wrapped around Travis's acreage, then Luke's property. Long enough for her to give herself a lecture about this visit. "You will be professional but supportive," she said as her little sedan crept along the dark driveway. "You haven't had any wine, so there's no excuse for a repeat of that embarrassing scene in the restaurant parking lot."

Even though she'd had a hard time forgetting their last kiss.

Her heart seemed to beat a little faster as she neared the house. Was he regretting the phone call? Was he looking forward to seeing her again? Doubtful. Mostly, he was worried, as any new father might be. He needed her wisdom, albeit limited, about children, and nothing else.

The porch light and the outdoor floodlight at the barn were on, welcoming her. She turned off the car engine and walked to the front door, just as she'd done for the past two weeks.

Only tonight felt different.

"You came," he said from the shadows of the doorway.

"I told you I would."

"I know, but it's not always easy to get away when you have a child, right?"

"That's true. One of the perks of living with your brother, however, is a built-in babysitter."

"That's one thing good about your brother."

She walked up to Luke. "Do you think you two will ever get along?"

"As in friends? Doubtful."

"Why?"

"I think it's obvious."

"Me?"

"What else? We don't exactly socialize."

"No, but you know some of the same people. Hank, for instance. He's Travis's best friend, and he's the reason you chose Ranger Springs when you were looking for land."

"True, and if I'm ever in the situation where Travis and I are at the same party at Hank's house, I'll be on my best behavior."

"But you won't like it."

"Hey, no offense, but your brother glares at me whenever he's within spitting distance."

"Crudely put, but effective."

Luke ran a hand through his hair. "I'm sorry. I didn't mean to be crude."

"That's okay. I know you're anxious and frustrated and just venting."

He smiled slightly. "Is that what I'm doing?"

"In my professional opinion, yes," she replied with a smile.

"You know, I think you just told me I'm having a hissy fit."

Kate laughed. "Where did you hear that term?"

"My mother used to say that a lot." He looked far into the night. "I'm really sorry she didn't live long enough to know about Brittany. She would have loved a grandchild."

"I'm sure she knew you'd get married someday and have children."

Luke shrugged. "Probably. I sure wasn't showing much promise in that area nine years ago."

"You were still awfully young then."

"Sometimes I don't think I've learned all that much about relationships and women since then."

"You have learned about relationships—with your daughter, I mean. I'm sure of it." She hoped she'd learned something from her own experiences lately—something that would keep her from thinking about kissing Luke again.

Luke looked at her as though he sensed her inner turmoil. "Come on inside and talk to me some more."

Chapter Thirteen

Kate entered the newly renovated and furnished living room with both interest and trepidation. The walls were painted a soft gold and the furniture sported neutral muslin slipcovers for easy washing, with colorful pillows. Robin had suggested some storage cubes that doubled as seating. Since Luke didn't own any personal items, she'd picked out prints and wall art that would look good in the ranch setting and wasn't too froufrou for a man.

"The living room looks great." Luke had turned on some of his new lamps, giving the room a warm glow. "It's hard to believe this room was so plain and bare just last week."

"What's hard to believe is all the work the contractor did in just two weeks. Everything is up to code, all nice and freshly painted. Nate Branson is a top-notch guy."

Luke had probably paid a premium price for such quick work, which showed where his priorities were—on his daughter, not his wallet. "Brittany will love the house."

"Do you think so? Really?"

His lingering insecurity touched Kate's heart. "She lives in an apartment now, right? This house is wonderful for her. Cozy and clean, surrounded by adorable animals. How could she not like it?"

"I worry because it's not grand, not like Travis's house, for example."

"Brittany won't miss something she's never had, Luke. Children don't covet the same way adults do."

"I don't covet your brother's house!"

She put her hand on his forearm. "I didn't mean that you did. I just wanted to assure you that comparing your house to someone else's won't enter her mind, at least not for a long time. At some point, she'll probably think a big new house would be neat."

"And then what do I do?"

Kate chuckled. "Either talk to her about appreciating the value of what you have…or buy her a new house."

"Very funny." He sounded a little sarcastic, but he smiled, so Kate did, too, and she felt the mood ease.

"Would you like something to drink? I made some iced tea earlier, and I have a bottle of wine chilled."

"I'm not sure I trust myself to drink wine around you," she admitted. Definitely not at night, in his cozy house.

"Then some tea? Or coffee?"

"Tea is fine." While Luke seemed more relaxed

right now, she was confident he would start thinking about Brittany's imminent arrival the moment she went home. And then he'd be just as stressed out as he'd been when he called. That meant they still needed to talk about what was really bothering him.

She wandered into the kitchen and watched him fill glasses with ice, pour tea and get the sweetener. He seemed nervous, as if they weren't here strictly to talk about his daughter. Like they were two adults, alone.

Kate took a steadying breath. "Luke, she truly is going to love it here. It's a nice community, even though that will be hard to adjust to at first. When she makes some new friends at school, she'll feel more comfortable. She'll love her new room and the house, plus the ranch and all the animals."

"I wonder if she'll accept me, though," he said as they settled on opposite ends of the couch. "I know you've gone over what to say when she asks the tough questions about her mother and me, about why I never contacted them, but what if she doesn't ask? What if she's so angry that she doesn't want to understand about my relationship with her mother?"

"For one thing, she doesn't need to know much about your relationship with Shawna. Focus on how kind her mother was to your mother—Brittany's grandmother—and you in that time of need. Tell her how much you appreciated Shawna going through your mother's things with you."

"I hope she does ask. That's one thing I can be totally truthful about."

Kate leaned forward. "She'll ask all those questions in her own time. Don't offer more than she's ready to hear. Just let her know that you'll discuss anything with her, but she needs to ask."

"You know so much about children." He smiled, looking devilishly handsome and yet so vulnerable in the golden glow of the lamps. "You know a lot about adults, too."

"Well, if I did, I'd have been more observant about what was going on around me."

"With your ex-husband?"

"Yes. He left everything behind, especially his family, to crawl into some hole somewhere and regroup."

"Someday he'll be sorry."

"Frankly, I don't give a damn," she said, setting her glass on the new coffee table. "But I'm ready to move on. I'm going to stop beating myself up about my stupid choices."

"You won't make the same mistakes twice."

"Lord, I hope not! After these past two weeks, I'm in much better shape financially. I'll get my own place as soon as I start getting regular paychecks. So thank you for hiring me. It's been a great experience."

"I couldn't have done this much without you, but I still have the hard part ahead of me, don't I?"

"Sorry, Luke. You called me over to talk about Brittany and I started in on my ex-husband and what a terrible father he is."

"I didn't call you only to talk about my situation. I just—" he shrugged and looked away "—called because when I got a little freaked out, I thought of how you could make sense of everything."

"I...I'm glad I could help."

"I felt anxious. But not since you arrived." He placed his glass next to hers and studied her face as if reading her thoughts.

"So you don't need to talk anymore?" She didn't know whether she should be relieved or worried that she didn't want to rush off. Before she allowed herself to go down that path, she jumped up from the couch. "I should be going, then. You probably have a lot to do tonight."

He rose also, moving closer. "Don't go. Not yet." With a subtle touch to her arm, he held her in place. "You make me feel good, Kate, and I think I make you feel good, too. Since we're not working together to get everything ready for Brittany anymore, can't we enjoy each other for now?"

Just for now? Or was he hinting that he wanted their relationship to change? Was he trying to seduce her? She didn't have much experience in that area, at least not in the past eight years. She swallowed and tried to keep the conversation light. "I haven't been drinking wine tonight. I'm pretty sure you'll be safe from me, but really, I shouldn't stay."

"But you want to," he added.

"I... Luke, this is not a good idea."

"Don't you get tired of doing the right thing all the time? Of always being sensible and following the rules?"

He apparently had no idea how often she'd been tempted by him. "I do try to do what's right."

"Then maybe I can convince you that this is right for us," he said in a sexy, dark voice as he slipped his arms around her, then pulled her against him. His lips pressed against her forehead, then beside her closed eyes. He smelled heavenly, like clean male and starch and a sexy aftershave. The blend of scents made her think of sun-bleached sheets and warm, aroused male.

Not that she'd experienced sun-bleached sheets with aroused males, at least in…well, never. "Just because this feels so good doesn't mean it's right," she whispered against his neck, longing to taste his skin and run her hands over his body and fill her senses with Luke.

She felt him smile, his lips turning up against her cheek as he kissed his way along her jawline. "If it feels so good, it can't be wrong," he said softly.

Yes, it could, she wanted to shout. She could barely breathe, and he wanted her to make a life-altering decision? He wanted her to act without weighing the repercussions? "What if we're making a huge mistake? What then?"

"Whatever you want. You tell me."

"I don't know." She couldn't tell him what she was feeling or thinking. She couldn't gaze into a crystal ball and see what would happen in one week, one month. She'd tried planning her life and see how well that had gone? She'd ended up divorced and barely supporting herself. Maybe there was something smart about going with what felt right now.

He tilted her chin with one hand as he continued to hold her close, and then he kissed her, hot and hungry and incredibly well. She gave everything to that kiss, wanting to mold herself to him, give herself to him. She felt overheated and needy, more than she'd ever felt before.

His hand drifted down her neck, across her chest to her breast. *Yes,* she silently urged. *Touch me there!* And then he did, his hand sculpting her, lifting her, and finally capturing her nipple between his fingers.

She moaned, but bit back a more earthy response as she twisted closer.

"Tell me what you want," he whispered against her ear, his breath tickling and arousing at the same time.

"I'm afraid," she admitted in a small voice.

"Afraid of me?" he asked incredulously.

"No! I'm…I'm afraid of myself. Of what I'm feeling."

"You don't need to be afraid. I would never ask you to do anything you don't want to do."

"But that's the problem. I want to do everything." She pulled back slightly to look at him. "Everything. Things I don't know anything about."

He swallowed, silent for once. She'd shocked him.

"I shouldn't have said that," she said quickly. "I shouldn't—"

"You should," he said, his expression and his tone fierce. "And you deserve everything." He kissed her again, taking her breath away. When he nibbled to a stop, he pulled back and smiled down at her. "You know so much, Kate. You know about children and adults, book learning and common sense galore. But I have a feeling in the area of romance, you need a little education."

"I think I need a lot of education," she answered breathlessly.

"And that's exactly what you're going to get." He bent and swept her into his arms.

She squealed and held on tight as he navigated around the couch, then strode down the hall with determined steps.

His bedroom was plain compared to the rest of the house, not yet decorated. Just a huge bed and curtains on the windows and that's all they needed anyway. He placed one knee on the mattress and lowered her gently as his mouth came down and kissed her again.

Then his body was stretched out alongside and over her, and all she felt was Luke, surrounding her with scent and sensation. Longing, deep and intense, swept through her.

"Tell me what you want," he whispered again as his hand swept her shirt upward.

"I want to feel your skin," she said, imagining his hot, smooth flesh against her own.

He swept her shirt away, leaving her lying on the bed in her plain white bra. Then he crossed his arms and lifted his own T-shirt, flinging it across the room.

Ed had neatly undressed in the closet, placing his clothes on the shelves or in the hamper. Never messy. Never so urgent and wild that he tossed his shirt aside.

But she didn't want to think about the past when she was here with Luke, and he looked incredible. All smooth, tight skin and muscle stretched over an amazing frame. He might have done stunts, but he looked like a movie star. Better than a movie star. He was real and he was here with her.

She ran her hands down his torso, loving the feel of him.

"I'm pretty tough," he said, confusing her, then he added, "You can touch me as much as you want. With your hands, your nails. Do whatever you want. It's all okay."

She did want to rake her nails down him. Not to hurt, but to claim him as her own.

No! He wasn't hers. She was just…borrowing him for the night. She closed her eyes and sunk into the sensations, pushing everything else out of her mind.

And then Luke lowered himself, kissing her, making her forget, and she held him tight. Some while later, perhaps minutes, perhaps hours, he broke away to finish undressing them both. She wasn't so sure about his seeing her naked. She'd had a baby, after all, and he was used to those hard-body California women. But it was fairly dark in here. Maybe he wouldn't notice her imperfections.

He didn't seem to care as he kissed his way down her body, over the faint stretch marks that probably weren't visible in the dim light but she knew were there. At the moment, they seemed incredibly sensitive. Or perhaps that was his undeniable ability to make her forget how much they didn't have in common and concentrate on only what they had together.

"You're beautiful, Kate," he said as he moved back up her body.

"I love to hear your voice," she admitted. "You make me feel so good."

"I'm going to make you feel even better."

"Teach me what I've been missing," she prompted.

He didn't need any more encouragement to reach for protection. Then, when she began an awkward attempt to sheath him in the condom, he finished the task with a smile. While she was still fascinated by the size and shape of him, he eased inside, stretching her, fitting them together so perfectly she felt tears threaten.

But as he began to move, fascination turned to passion. Deep, deep passion. She needed no more instruction. Her body knew what she wanted, knew how to respond and give and take until she couldn't think any longer. She arched off the bed, crying his name and scoring his back as her world exploded. She barely heard him moan her name, but she felt his shudders as he held her tight.

Sometime later, they both moved, adjusted their bodies so she could breathe and he could rid himself of the condom. He didn't leave her, though. He snuggled to her and smoothed her hair and told her she was beautiful.

Kate smiled against his smooth, hot chest. Luke was amazing. This was addictive. She could do this forever.

Her eyes opened as reality began seeping into her consciousness like the cool night air on her heated skin. This wasn't forever. She couldn't be addicted to Luke Simon. His daughter was arriving tomorrow, she had a six-year-old son at home, and she'd promised herself their attraction was just about the moment. She wasn't ready for a relationship, would probably never be ready for a man like Luke Simon, who made her feel wonderful and confused at the same time.

What had she done?

LUKE SAVORED the feel of Kate, all warm and soft, curled beside him, as he drifted between awareness and sleep. For a moment after they'd made love, he was afraid she would jump up and run away. She'd seemed tense, her breathing irregular. But as he'd held her and told her how wonderful she was, she'd relaxed.

He hadn't planned to make love to Kate tonight. He'd truly been anxious about Brittany's arrival tomorrow. But when he'd seen her on his new couch, remembered how she'd sincerely cared about his success these past two weeks, he wanted to take their friendship to the next level.

He was surprised she hadn't run screaming out the door when he'd touched her. He wasn't the best choice for a…a what? He didn't even know what to call their relationship. And what had he been thinking anyway, he reminded himself as his brain cleared and adrenaline kicked in. Kate had come over to help him through a moment of panic. She hadn't come over to get seduced. He'd talked her into that kiss, then carried her off to bed.

Dammit, he'd fallen into his old bachelor routine. He'd been charming. He'd said the right things. He'd gotten the girl.

But this "girl" wasn't someone from a Hollywood set or a smoky bar. This was Kate Wooten, schoolteacher and mother. How many times had he told himself that Kate was a forever kind of woman, that she deserved a man who could give her the life she'd left behind?

Luke didn't know anything about family life. He knew horses and movie sets and hard work.

Although he and his mother had been family, he'd never known what it was like to have a father. He wouldn't know how to be a traditional father or husband. Would he? The concept shook him more than he wanted to admit, even to himself. And it reinforced his idea that until he was sure he could succeed as a father, he shouldn't rush into a serious relationship with Kate, no matter how much he wanted her in his bed. It wasn't fair to her, or to Eddie, who'd already lost one dad.

"Are you asleep?" Kate asked.

He'd started to move his arm from around her naked shoulders, hoping to get up without disturbing her. "Ah, no, I was just thinking?"

"Oh. About…this?"

He couldn't admit he was starting to panic, that he shouldn't have made love with her, so he slipped back into the one thing he and Kate had in common. "I was thinking about Brittany coming home tomorrow."

"That has a nice ring to it, doesn't it?"

"It sure does." Home, he could handle. Family was the word he had trouble with.

She moved a little, probably because her arm was asleep. "Luke, there's one thing you really need to consider, something I've mentioned before but we haven't talked much about."

He didn't like the sound of where she was going. "What?"

"This community is close-knit, even the newer folks who have moved in. They are warm and welcoming, and they don't understand when someone doesn't embrace them as well. If you don't join in, they might misinterpret your motives, or assume that you have something to hide."

"I'm not hiding anything! I've been going to the café more, shopping in town, and greeting everyone I know." He'd done everything he could think of to be polite and neighborly. Just because he didn't talk about his personal life, his background, to everyone he met didn't mean he was being secretive.

"I'm just mentioning this because some people still don't feel as if they know you. Even when you do come into town, you don't share much news or information with them."

He pulled his arm from around Kate and swung his legs over the side of the bed. "Good grief! I've been busy. Besides, I'm not going to pour out my pedigree—or lack of one—to the citizens of Ranger Springs."

"They aren't asking for a pedigree. They just want to know you, the Luke Simon who lives among them and buys from Branson's Hardware and the grocery store and Robin's Nest. They want to understand why you chose to live here, why you have the animals, what you plan to do with them."

"I simply plan to give them a home for as long as they live. It's not complicated!"

"Then why don't you say so?"

He rose from the bed and paced the darkness of the room, running a hand through his hair. "Because…because it's none of their damn business. I'm not asking them for money. I'm paying my taxes and keeping my property in good condition."

"That's not all they're interested in."

He turned to Kate and put his hands on his naked hips. "I know what they want. They want to make sure I'm one of them. Well, I'm not. I'm the bastard child of a single, working-class mother who would have given anything to be a part of this community. But she wasn't. She worked two jobs to support us. She did not have time to sit around the café, drink coffee and eat pie and talk about what her neighbors are doing."

"Luke, that's not fair! That's not what this community is all about, and it's not what most people do."

"Oh, yeah? That's what everyone was doing the day I rode into town. That's what a lot of them are doing when I go anywhere around the square."

"You think they're talking about you?"

"I think they must be doing some talking about me, or you wouldn't have brought up the subject."

"This is a ridiculous conversation," Kate said, throwing the sheet over her body, pulling it loose and wrapping it around her like a toga as she swung her legs over the side of the bed. "I brought up the subject because I knew you were anxious about Brittany's arrival. She'll need to be accepted by the community, which means that you need to be accepted, which means that *you* need to get rid of that attitude and be more friendly. But if you don't want to do that, just remember you're only hurting your daughter."

"You know I wouldn't do anything to hurt her."

"You'll hurt her by your stubborn denial that anyone is interested in knowing you as a person. If you don't want to be friendly, then fine. I'm not going to lecture you."

"That's good, because this schoolteacher act is a little odd considering we're both naked!"

"Well, that will be remedied shortly, and believe me, it won't happen again!"

She grabbed her clothes from where he'd strewn them across the floor and made a dash for the bathroom. He didn't say anything as she left his bedroom. Maybe it was best that she was angry. They didn't belong together and he should never have made her think, even for a moment, that they did.

Chapter Fourteen

The outdoor lights cast shadows across the drive, but all the lamps were off inside Travis and Jodie's house as Kate pulled to a stop in front of the garage. Good. She didn't want to face anyone right now, especially her know-it-all brother. She certainly didn't want him to take one look at her and shout, "I told you so!"

Travis might have been right about her avoiding a personal relationship with Luke, but he'd been wrong about Luke not being a good man. He was. He was also such an incredibly hardheaded reverse-snob that she wondered why she'd missed that part of his personality up until now. Had she chosen to close her eyes, or had she been too focused on some other aspect of his life? Or maybe she'd downplayed the importance of that chip on his shoulder. Whatever she'd done, it had come back to bite her on the rear end.

The fact that he was a good man at heart only slightly alleviated the hurt she felt now, knowing she'd made another bad call involving men. She'd known she should wait, that she shouldn't rush into a relationship on the heels of her divorce.

But had she listened to her own words of wisdom? No, of course not. At the first opportunity, she'd placed her arms around Luke's neck and let him carry her off to bed. Making love was one more error in judgment...but oh, it had been a glorious, wonderful experience while it lasted.

Shaking herself out of those memories, she vowed that she wouldn't dwell on her mistakes with Luke. After she got her teaching job, she'd make new memories. She wouldn't allow herself to obsess over Luke. She knew he'd move on. When she was all settled into her new house or apartment, he'd barely remember their one and only night together. He'd forgotten Brittany's mother easily enough.

She wished she could forget him, but that was impossible, at least for now. Her mind kept going back to their time together, back to that final conversation.

Whatever reasons Luke had for avoiding involvement in the community, Brittany would suffer the consequences. Kate had wanted to make Luke understand that important point. As soon as her emotions cooled, she'd make another attempt for Brittany's sake. Maybe in writing this time.

But no more romance between herself and Luke. She couldn't go through those feelings of elation and letdown again, not after caring about him and his daughter for two long weeks. Not after sharing kisses and being swept into his bedroom and lying naked in his arms. Not after he made her wanton and needy and wild beyond her experience.

Yes, she'd made a mistake, but she wasn't going to beat herself up. She'd learned something about herself tonight. She felt like a woman again, for which she was grateful. Luke's hardheadedness couldn't take that confidence away.

Taking a deep breath to center herself, she exited the car, closing the door as quietly as possible. She'd pick up Eddie tomorrow morning since there was no reason to wake him right now.

The night was perfectly still and the gentle click of the car door latch seemed loud and intrusive. As she began to climb the stairs, her legs felt as heavy as her heart. She reached the landing after what seemed an eternity, inserted her key and then, thinking she might not have turned off the headlights, she looked over the railing to check. The only light she saw was one in the main house's kitchen. She hoped it was Jodie.

No such luck. Travis was silhouetted in the window; she knew that he saw her standing up here, dragging home in the wee hours of the morning.

She'd hear about this tomorrow. With a sigh, she waved at her overprotective brother and entered her apartment.

TRAVIS TOOK his usual table by the front window of the Four Square Café, forcing a smile as he greeted his friends and neighbors. Ambrose and Joyce

Wheatley came in around eight-thirty, with Thelma
Rogers arriving shortly thereafter. The women were
all abuzz about something—Travis hoped they
weren't discussing his sister's late-night rendezvous with Luke Simon—and giggled like teenage
girls. Charlene Jacks rushed off to a booth near the
back, where Nate Branson sat drinking coffee. He
was a handsome, middle-aged man, still lean and
fit. Charlene adjusted her blouse, smoothed her
sassy recent haircut and slid in opposite the new
man in town.

Well, well. Romance was alive and well in Ranger Springs. Good for Charlene. She'd raised three
daughters by herself, ever since her husband had quit
her. He'd died a few years later, and the girls were all
doing well. They'd even purchased the café for Charlene a few years ago. Now she still waited tables, but
she owned this place and the Prince Alexi Museum
housed above, a tribute to one of her sons-in-law.

These good people would be great for Kate, if she
didn't get involved with that loner Luke Simon. He'd
pretty much holed up on his property for the past few
weeks and the only ones who knew why were Kate
and Robin Parker, wife of the chief of police. Robin
was good at keeping secrets, and Kate wasn't about
to tell tales about Luke Simon. For some reason, she
felt real protective of the outsider.

She'd even refused to talk about her late-night
jaunt over to his place to "talk." Yeah, right. He'd
seen the look of wounded pride—and also the love

bite on her neck—when she'd come over this morning to get Eddie. Something had happened last night at Simon's house, and Travis felt like taking out his frustrations on his new neighbor.

Not that he was a violent man. But his sister was vulnerable. She needed protection despite her assurances that she was okay without his help.

"More coffee?" The waitress refilled his cup at his nod. He eased his hand out of the fist he'd made as he watched Hank saunter into the café.

"'Bout time you showed up."

"Hey, my lady needed me this morning. What can I say?" his friend replied with a suggestive smile.

"To take out the trash, maybe."

"I've got other skills." Hank grinned. "She needed me to hang a new curtain in the baby's room."

Travis rolled his eyes. "It's a sad day when Hank McCauley is reduced to an interior-decorating assistant."

He shrugged. "The perks are pretty good." Hank motioned the waitress over and asked for coffee, then added, "I hear your sister's been helping out Luke. Is that work about finished?"

Travis's hand tightened around his coffee mug handle. "Finished is a good word for it. If she never goes over there again, it will be too soon for me."

"Hey, what's up? I thought you'd mellowed out about Luke."

"He put the moves on her last night. She came home late. I'm pretty sure they had some sort of argument. I swear, Hank, I felt like... Look, I know he's your friend, but he'd better not hurt my sister."

Hank held up his hand. "I don't know anything about that. Luke's really close-lipped about his personal life."

"Yeah, well, he'd better keep his lips to himself. As of now, I'm making my sister off-limits."

"Uh, Travis, that kind of ultimatum doesn't work well with women."

"I'm not talking about women! I'm talking about Luke Simon."

"So you're going to go over to his ranch, full of brotherly self-righteousness, and tell him to stay away from your womenfolk?" Hank shrugged. "Give yourself a few days to cool off, then go over there and talk to him like a rational adult. Stop acting all outraged."

"I'm not acting!" And okay, maybe he needed to cool off a little before he talked to Luke Simon.

"Good thing," Hank said, smiling up at the waitress who'd brought him coffee. "You'd never get an Oscar for that performance."

LUKE STOOD at the gate in the San Antonio airport, waiting for Brittany. The person at the reservation counter had told him that a flight attendant would escort her off the plane and he'd have to show his ID. He had out his new Texas driver's license, along with a copy of Brittany's birth certificate, just in case.

As he waited, he looked down at the typing on the slip; the name change wasn't official yet. His last name was incorrectly listed as "Moretti," but that would be corrected soon. Then he and Brittany would officially be a family, just like he and his mother had been a family.

If only he'd known Shawna had gotten pregnant. He didn't have much back then, but he would have done whatever he could, including marrying her if that had been what she wanted, to make sure his child had two parents who loved her. But he didn't have that chance, and now he had to make up for those eight years. Now he had more experience, more money and, hopefully, more maturity.

Not that he'd shown much maturity last night, when he'd seduced the woman who'd helped him get ready for his daughter, who'd coached him on how to be a father and pretty much guided the changes he'd made for Brittany.

There, in the passageway coming from the plane, he saw Brittany walking beside a tall, slender African-American woman. They were talking, Brittany smiling shyly and holding her backpack. She looked like Shawna, with sun-streaked brown hair, but Brittany had his dark eyes. Someday she'd be striking. He'd have to make sure she understood that teenaged boys were up to no good.

You hadn't been up to any good with Kate last night, had you? his conscience asked. He pushed the reminders of his mistake aside as Brittany stopped in the gate area.

"Hello, Brittany," he said, smiling as he stepped

forward. He felt a lump in his throat, a heavy thumping in his chest, when he looked into the eyes of the
flight attendant and said, "I'm her father."

AS SOON AS Brittany got acquainted with the house,
barn and animals—which to Luke's relief she
loved—she started asking questions. Obvious questions, such as where had Luke lived before? Poignant questions, such as where did the animals come
from and were they going to stay here forever, or
would Luke send them away? He almost grabbed her
and hugged her tight when she asked that one. And
more difficult ones, about whether he'd loved her
mother and why didn't they live together when she
was a baby?

Thankfully, Kate had gone over many of these
questions with him, anticipating Brittany's curiosity
about his past and her role in his life now. He might
have come off as too cautious in his answers, but he
hoped she understood that he was getting used to
being a father.

As he got accustomed to the newly decorated
house along with Brittany, he saw Kate in every
room. She'd helped him pick out the furniture and accessories and consulted on paint colors that were either soothing or stimulating to young minds. She
used words like that naturally, because she was a
natural teacher. A natural mother, too. *And not the
woman for him.*

On the second day, when Brittany asked if there

were any other children to play with, he debated whether he could call Kate and ask her if Eddie could come over. This was spring break, so Eddie had the time off. If Kate wasn't too angry with him, she'd bring her son over. If nothing else, then to see the new miniature horses, the little mare named Precious and the foal that Brittany had yet to name.

Names were very important, she'd told him with a serious expression on her face. She couldn't rush into naming the "pony" because he would have that name forever. Luke wondered if she'd been thinking about her own name, first Moretti and now Simon. No doubt Shawna had also had to explain why she had yet a different last name. The idea twisted his heart; one more thing he felt guilty about.

While Brittany sat in the living room and read one of the books Kate had chosen, he decided to put aside his doubts and call her to ask about Eddie.

"Kate, this is Luke," he said when she answered.

"Oh." He heard the surprise in her voice. "Hello." She sounded chilly. "Is everything okay?"

"Brittany's fine." He took a deep breath, wondering if he should say something about what had happened two nights ago. He didn't know what to say, so he decided to stick to talking about his daughter—the reason he had a relationship of any sort with Kate in the first place. "She was asking about other kids to play with, and since I don't know anyone else with kids—" which might just be a commentary on what Kate was telling him the night they'd made love "—I wondered if Eddie could come over to play."

Kate hesitated for a moment, then said, "I'll bring him over in about half an hour."

He was about to tell her he'd be glad to pick Eddie up, but she hung up after a hasty, "Goodbye."

Okay, fine. She had good reason to still be angry. He'd been a little abrupt that night, but she didn't know the whole story. No one here did, not even Hank.

Telling everyone about his past was too uncomfortable. Luke really didn't want them to know who his father was or how he'd gotten the money to buy the land and support the animals. A little knowledge led to more curiosity, and before he knew it, he and his late mother would be fodder for gossip. He might be plagued by someone like the author who was doing a biography on Ronald Lucas Simon, when all Luke wanted was peace and quiet.

Kate wanted him to be completely open about himself, but if he was, he'd hurt Brittany by shining a spotlight on her. Not only would she be the new kid in school, but also the illegitimate child of an illegitimate child. Being a bastard didn't have the same connotations now that it did thirty years ago, but that didn't mean he should air the family linen.

He wouldn't do anything to hurt Brittany. Knowing that her grandfather was a deceitful, womanizing SOB and that Brittany had aunts, uncles and cousins she would never know would *not* help her settle into her new life.

No, he'd keep quiet about his family secrets. If Kate couldn't live with that…

He didn't know what he'd do. Even with Brittany here, he felt as if he had a big hole in his life—a hole that Kate had filled for two weeks before he'd gone and messed up their relationship with sex.

KATE FELT nervous anticipation that she tried not to convey to Eddie as she steered down the driveway toward Luke's house. She wasn't ready to see Luke yet, but his plea to bring Eddie over had hit a chord. Everything she'd done for the past two weeks—with the exception of making love to Luke in a moment of insanity—had been for Brittany. How could Kate, in good conscience, deny her a playmate?

Eddie bounced with excitement at the prospect of meeting the much-talked-about Brittany. Also, she was older, so that gave her much more appeal in his six-year-old mind. Playing with the older kids was always cool.

Kate pulled to a stop between the house and barn. As soon as she cut the engine and opened the door, she heard voices from the barn. Apparently Luke and his daughter were either looking at or taking care of the animals.

Excited yips greeted her as she walked past the Jack Russell terriers in their shaded run beside the barn. Eddie ran over to pet them through the chain links. The dogs jumped up and down on their hind legs like they had springs attached. She smiled, watched Eddie with them, and thought that as soon as she got a new place, she'd get him a dog or a puppy. She'd have to ask Luke which would be more appropriate.

Her smile faded. No, that was just the type of thinking that led her to be dependent on others. On men. She could make her own decisions about pets. About everything.

"Come on, Eddie. I'm sure Brittany wants to meet you."

"Okay, Mommy." He ran toward the barn door, full speed ahead like most boys his age. Seeing him act so healthy and normal made her happy, because for some time he'd been so upset by the divorce and his father's desertion.

"Hi, Mr. Simon," he said cheerfully from inside the barn. Kate stepped from the light into the shade and let her eyes adjust. Luke stood beside the stall of the miniature horses, looking so good in a pair of worn jeans, a plaid shirt and scuffed boots. His skin was tan, his eyes bright with emotion as he saw her. Interest or lingering animosity? Kate wasn't sure and reminded herself not to care. She'd helped Luke, he had his daughter. The end.

Brittany stood on the bottom board, taller than Kate had expected. Kate walked forward with a smile to greet the little girl she'd heard so much about.

"You must be Brittany," she said, bending slightly at the waist to be at eye level. "I've heard so many wonderful things about you from your daddy. I'm Ms. Wooten and this is my son Eddie."

Eddie bounced forward and grinned. "Hi. I'm only six, but Mommy said we could play together. I love all the animals, especially the zebras. What do you like?"

Brittany seemed overwhelmed for a moment, then smiled shyly and said, "I like the little horses."

"Brittany hasn't named the foal yet," Luke told Kate. "I told her you named the mare—the mother."

"Yes, I did," Kate said to Brittany, avoiding Luke's scrutiny. She wanted this to be about Brittany, not him. "Have you thought of a name for the baby horse?"

Brittany shook her head. "No, not yet."

"I was just about to turn them out into their pasture. Would you and Brittany like to watch?" Luke asked Eddie.

"Yeah!"

"Go outside and stand by the fence, then, and maybe the mare will run outside."

Both children ran for the door, already competitive as Eddie giggled and tried to beat Brittany to the sunlight.

Just as Kate began to follow the children, Luke put his hand on her shoulder and gently pulled her back. She turned to face him, her heart beating fast and her breathing shallow. She thought she might hyperventilate.

"Thank you for coming," he said softly. "I wasn't sure you would."

"I wanted to meet Brittany," she said, ignoring her reaction to Luke.

"I see." His gaze searched her face, looking for the truth.

"I'm doing my best to be friends," she admitted finally. "I want your daughter to feel welcome. I want my son to believe that you're not angry with us."

"I'm not angry." He glanced down, then back up. "I'm sorry I got angry the other night. You hit a nerve."

"I said what I thought was necessary."

"I'm thinking about it, but it's complicated."

Kate stiffened. "Yes, it's easy for things to get complicated when there's usually a simple answer."

"What's that supposed to mean?"

"That night was a mistake. We should have remained friends. That is, if you ever considered me a friend."

"You know I did."

"Luke," she said, stepping back from him, "I'm not sure what I know about you anymore."

He looked at her intensely, his face stark in the muted light of the barn. His lips parted, as if he wanted to say something else, and she held her breath. Then he looked away and said, "We should get back to the kids. That's why we're here, right?"

"Right," Kate answered, wondering why she'd even momentarily thought she could handle a romantic relationship with him, one that would lead to something more serious than either of them were ready for, now or ever.

She'd spent seven years with a man she didn't really know. She'd told herself she wasn't going to make the same mistake again. Then she'd jumped into bed with Luke, throwing all her well-conceived plans right out the window.

As she stood there and tortured herself by watching Luke, he turned and unlatched the stall door, speaking gently to the miniature horses. She heard him open the door to the outside pen and the snort of the mare. Only then did she turn and walk outside to the excited chatter of the children and the thunder of eight tiny hooves.

Chapter Fifteen

Somehow Kate managed to get through the nearly two hours she spent at Luke's ranch. Brittany and Eddie got along fairly well, considering their difference in age. Brittany enjoyed her welcome gift, a tiny circus carousel, which Eddie explained had zebras people could actually ride. She and Luke, however, never overcame the tension, the unspoken rift between them.

She and Luke didn't set up another day for the children to play. He had to get Brittany ready to start school the next Monday. Kate should have made arrangements for Eddie to see his grandparents—his maternal grandmother in Palm Springs or his maternal grandfather in Hilton Head—but she'd been so busy with Luke she hadn't made plans for spring break.

She would have allowed him to see his paternal grandparents, but ever since the divorce and Ed's disappearance from their lives, they "couldn't" see their grandchild. It was too painful, they'd explained, but they didn't consider that it was even more painful to Eddie to lose both his father and his grandparents.

On Wednesday, with Jodie, Travis and Marsha in California, Kate decided she and Eddie couldn't stay around the apartment any longer. She made a spur-of-the-moment decision to take Eddie to the zoo in San Antonio. He loved animals; he should be reminded that they lived somewhere other than Luke Simon's ranch.

Maybe they should invite Brittany to go along.

She started to pick up the phone, but stopped herself. She wasn't ready to talk to him or, even worse, have him insist he go along for his daughter's sake. So she told Eddie that just the two of them would go to the zoo.

They had a fun day seeing the animals, then stopped for dinner at one of Eddie's favorite pizza restaurants on the north side of the city. When she came out to drive back to Ranger Springs, the sun had already set.

"Brittany would have liked the animals and the pizza," Eddie said, sighing dramatically from the back seat.

"I had fun with you," Kate said cheerfully. When he didn't respond, she added, "Perhaps you and Brittany can go to the zoo some other time."

"With Mr. Simon, too?"

No, she thought to herself. "I'm not sure."

"I like him and his ranch. It's fun over there."

Kate felt like sighing just as dramatically as she

looked in the rearview mirror at her son. "When we move into our own house or apartment after the new school year starts, I'll bet we have a lot of fun, too."

"I like living with Uncle Travis and Aunt Jodie."

"They've been really nice, but we'll have our own place."

"We could move to Luke's ranch."

"No, we can't. He has just enough room for Brittany."

Eddie folded his arms over his chest. "He could make room for us."

"Eddie, that isn't going to happen." Saying the words out loud made them much more final.

"It could."

"No, it couldn't." She turned on the radio. She didn't want to ruin the day for her son, and she didn't want to think about Luke anymore. She thought about him enough without reminders from her six-year-old.

WHEN BRITTANY WENT to school on Monday, Luke felt as though he was sending her off to kindergarten for the first day rather than to second grade. After he drove her to school, walked her inside and was assured by the teacher that everything would be fine, he went back out to his truck and sat in front of the school, brooding. He supposed he was more nervous than his daughter. He wished he could be there each moment to help her through the unfamiliar school, the strangers. He didn't mind going to new places where he didn't know anyone, but he wasn't eight years old.

Kate had told him that Brittany would need to be accepted by the community, which meant the kids in school as well as adults she might meet. He realized that now, thinking about her sitting alone at her desk in an unfamiliar classroom.

Kate had also told him that *he* needed to be accepted. She'd even said that he needed to change his attitude and be more friendly. She said that if he didn't do that, he would be hurting his daughter.

Dammit, he realized, punching the steering wheel with his palm, Kate was right. He needed to do something fast to fit into this community. But what?

WHEN LUKE CALLED to see if Brittany could come over to play after school and asked if Travis or Jodie could watch the children so they could talk, Kate almost fell off her kitchen chair. She hadn't heard from him and wondered each day if she ever would again, and then he called with such an unusual request. Luke didn't even like Travis, and he was asking him to babysit!

Since he'd wanted to talk in private, she followed him back to his ranch and parked behind his pickup. The day was warm and bright, hinting of summer to come, but she felt like shivering when she stepped into his living room.

"Would you like some iced tea? A soda?" Luke asked as Kate placed her purse on the end of the couch.

"No, thank you. I'd like to know why you suddenly needed to talk."

He took a deep breath. "I realized that what you'd told me had a lot of merit. I should have listened. I shouldn't have overreacted." He shrugged. "I guess people do have a right to know who's living near them."

"Yes, and I'm sure they'll like both you and Brittany once they get to know you. But why did you feel obligated to tell me this privately?"

"You've helped me so much Kate that I...I wanted to explain everything to you first."

"First?"

Luke shrugged. "I need to start someplace."

"I see." But she didn't, not really. Luke was treating her as though she were just any friend. Hank, the waitresses at the café, his helper Carlos. Not the woman he'd gotten naked with and made love to and lay beside in the dark of night.

"I need to tell you how I got the money to open the ranch. I was a little secretive about that before. Before you confronted me about living here, I guess I was in denial. I mean, Hank had mentioned something similar about blending into the community, but I wasn't ready to listen. And really, I didn't think it mattered, that it should matter, to anyone. I didn't get it illegally or immorally."

Kate hugged her arms around herself as though protecting herself from the feelings and memories of this room, of being carried down the hall and laid on his bed. She settled into the end of the couch. Luke sat near but not touching and pulled a piece of paper toward her.

"What's this?" There were lines and circles, some of them filled in with names, in a stick-tree style.

"My feeble attempt to make a family tree for Brittany."

Luke watched Kate's expression change from wary and wounded to what he now thought of as "schoolteacher mode." "No, you've done a good job. This will give her a feeling of roots, of permanence. That's important after all she's been through."

"Yeah, well, there's not much there," he admitted. Brittany had asked about his mother and father, aunts and uncles, cousins and nieces and nephews. He'd stumbled around the subject so much that she'd gotten all sad and he'd heard her sobbing in her room, so he'd promised they'd work on a family tree.

His family. What a joke. He didn't know these people. Brothers and sisters? Maybe by blood, on his father's side, but they didn't mean anything to him. They didn't acknowledge him; he didn't seek them out.

He would never seek them out.

Kate frowned, staring at the paper. "Your father is Ronald Lucas Simon? There's a famous children's museum in Kansas City named for him. I remember getting educational materials from there when I did my student teaching."

Luke nodded. He didn't think it would be so painful to talk about his past. "He never acknowledged me while he was alive, even though he knew my mother was pregnant."

"That's terrible! He seemed so upstanding."

"Yeah, well, I wouldn't hold him up as someone special, based on what I know about the man. I'm not exactly overjoyed that he's my biological father."

Kate put her hand on his arm as she had when they worked together. "Because he didn't marry your mother?"

Something snapped inside of him. He tried to hold it in, to calm himself down, but he couldn't.

"That bastard not only didn't marry my mother, he couldn't, because he was already married. He had a wife—someone from his own wealthy world—and kids who went to private schools. That wasn't enough for him. He had to seduce Angela Moretti, a teenager who walked dogs at the hotel where he stayed, for God's sake. And you know why she was walking dogs? She wanted to earn money for vet school."

"Oh, no."

"Oh, yes. And you know the strangest thing? She loved him anyway. He ruined her life! She never graduated from high school, much less went to vet school. Not with a baby and no means of support after her parents kicked her out."

Kate swallowed and he saw unshed tears in her eyes. "And when he found out about you?"

"He claimed I wasn't his at first, but then he said that even if I was, I wasn't his responsibility. He and my mother didn't have a 'relationship,' he claimed. He paid her hospital bill, gave her a little money and told her not to contact him again."

"Oh, Luke, I'm sorry."

"I don't want your pity!" He shook off her arm and paced the room. "My mother didn't want your pity. She didn't even want his undying affection and complete loyalty. All she wanted was a little piece of his life. She was willing to settle for a smidgen of his love, but he couldn't even give her that."

"I think," Kate said slowly, "that you're really angry because he wouldn't give *you* any time or acknowledgment."

"You're wrong, Kate. I'm angry that my mother wasted her life over the love of a man who didn't love her back."

Kate felt as though Luke had yelled those words at her, to shake her up until she experienced his pain. She relived her own experience. She'd wasted seven years, not her whole life over a man. She'd assumed everything was fine. She'd pushed her doubts under her fine Oriental rugs and rushed out the door to Eddie's soccer practice, oblivious that her world was falling down.

And given a little encouragement, she might fall into the same routine with Luke. If he would just define their relationship, give her hope of a future, she'd wait and wait. And maybe it would never happen. Maybe he'd always have another priority, another crisis.

But this conversation wasn't about her. She had to pull herself together.

Luke frowned at her. "Are you okay?"

"I'm fine. I just…I suppose I got a little too empathetic there for a moment." She took a deep breath. "I'm sorry if I seemed as though I was psychoanalyzing you."

"I've thought about this my whole life, Kate. I loved my mother, but she was blind when it came to Ronald Simon. And yes, maybe I'm a little angry at her, but she's gone."

"Yes, and so is your…so is Ronald Lucas Simon."

"Yes, he is. He died, and in his will, he left me, the 'unnamed illegitimate offspring,' five million dollars."

Kate felt her eyes widen. She didn't know what to say. All those times when she'd wondered if Luke had enough money to pay for the remodeling popped into her head, but she didn't say anything.

"Of course, that was a fraction of what he left his legitimate family—not that they didn't resent the bequest—but I wasn't expecting even a dollar. It was quite a surprise, to say the least."

"I'm sure it was."

"I wasn't sure I would accept his money at first, but then I got to thinking about what I could do with it. Something that would make my mother proud. Something that Ronald Lucas Simon would never have expected."

"Oh, Luke."

"Kate, I don't spend a dime of his money on me.

I've made enough to keep me and Brittany comfortable for a long time. The inheritance is for the animals, to give them a future when they had none. To give them hope when they were lost and lonely and tired." He looked out the window to the newly green pastures and swaying trees. "My mother would have loved this place. She would have loved this town."

Kate felt tears in her eyes again, but this time they were about Luke and the mother he'd lost, and the love Angela had never truly realized. Kate reached out and held Luke, hugging him tight as he buried his head in her neck and held her back. They stayed that way for quite a while, until she heard him sniff and felt him wipe away a tear.

"Kate—"

She couldn't stay. She had to leave. "I hate to rush off, but I'd better get back to Brittany and Eddie. I don't want to impose on Travis and Jodie too long."

"Kate, there's one more thing." He waited until she put her purse back down, then continued. "Someone is writing a book about Ronald Simon. He's been trying to find out who that 'unnamed offspring' in the will is. One of the reasons I was so secretive at first is because I didn't want him to find me. I realize now that I have no control over someone writing a book. I still don't want him to find *us*."

"No, that wouldn't be good for Brittany."

"I hope you can understand why I thought it was best to keep to myself."

"I know that this town won't do anything to take

advantage of who you are or why you're here. They can keep secrets. I've heard stories involving a prince that fell in love with a local girl...but that's beside the point."

"The point is that I'm planning something big to introduce Brittany, me and the animals to Ranger Springs."

"That's wonderful, Luke. I know you'll find everyone very accepting."

He frowned. "Why aren't you asking what I've planned?"

"I'm sure you can do this on your own."

"I didn't mean that I wanted you to help me again."

She felt as if he'd slapped her. "I'm sorry. I didn't mean to suggest you needed my help."

He strode toward her, crowding the space near the front door. Her escape. "Kate, you've been great," he said, his voice low. Then he frowned again and stepped back slightly. "I mean, you've been a great friend. The best. I can't thank you enough for all your help with me, the house and Brittany."

She swallowed her pain. "You're welcome. Now, I really must go. I'll ask Jodie to drive Brittany home." Anything to keep from seeing Luke again.

Kate placed her hand on the knob, then paused. "You've done a great thing, Luke. You should never feel awkward or reserved about explaining the situation to anyone."

And then she escaped out the front door before their tentative friendship was tested...again.

LUKE WAVED to Jodie as she pulled away from the house, then turned his attention to Brittany. "Did you have a good time playing with Eddie?"

"Yes, but he doesn't have any animals. Oh, and they have a baby."

Luke smiled. "Yes, I know."

"I think I like animals better."

"That's good." Because there weren't going to be any babies around here. No human babies, at least. Not unless he married, and he didn't see that happening. Especially since he had gone to great lengths to establish his relationship with Kate as "just friends."

No matter how difficult, he'd stuck to his priorities: keep their relationship neighborly, not sexual and get Brittany accepted in the community. Besides, Kate wasn't looking for anything serious. She kept saying how she wanted to be on her own, get her own place. She was so happy when she heard she had a job in the Ranger Springs elementary school. She didn't want any more from him than a neighborly, cordial relationship.

So why did he keep seeing the hurt expression in her eyes when he'd thanked her and said she was a good friend?

He had to shake himself out of these thoughts. "Did I tell you about the potbellied pigs?" he asked Brittany.

"Pigs? Are we going to get pigs?"

"Next week. An animal rescue group will bring us two who need homes. One is black and one has spots."

"Really? Oh, thank you...Daddy," she said for the

first time. Daddy. She'd called him "Luke" before this moment. He felt as if she'd punched him, and still, he couldn't keep a huge grin off his face.

He put his arm around Brittany and steered her into the house. He would quit thinking about Kate, except as a friend. And he had to get ready to introduce himself, his daughter and his animals to the people of Ranger Springs.

A FEW DAYS LATER Travis handed Kate the local paper. "I thought you might want to see this."

Puzzled, she took the slightly crumpled newspaper from her brother. "What did you want to show me?"

"Just look at the third page." He paused, then shook his head. "I'll see you later."

Kate closed the screen door, then unfolded the *Springs Gazette* while she walked into the living room. "Oh my gosh," she said softly as she sat on the couch. "I never thought he'd do *this*."

"What, Mommy?"

"It's an ad for everyone in town to come to see Mr. Simon's ranch."

Eddie scampered over and bounced beside her on the couch. "Read it to me!"

She gave her son her best schoolteacher glare.

"Pleeeze."

"Okay." She settled Eddie closer. "'You are cordially invited to the Last Chance Ranch on Sunday afternoon from two o'clock to four o'clock to meet

Luke Simon, his daughter Brittany and their four-legged friends.'"

"Look, there's Lollipop!" Eddie exclaimed, pointing to one of the photos arranged down the side of the page.

"Yes, I think all the animals are there." This was the event he'd tried to tell her about when they'd talked, which she tried not to dwell on while her son waited impatiently for her to continue reading. "The invitation also says that there will be refreshments. No donations will be accepted."

"What does that mean about no donations?"

"That means Mr. Simon doesn't want anyone to give him money for the animals."

"Like selling them?"

"No, like for their feed and vet bills," Kate replied absently. She understood now why he'd never seemed concerned about money, despite being "retired" at the age of thirty. She understood a lot of things about him, but his sharing of his past hadn't brought them closer. No, he'd made sure she knew they were just friends. Neighbors. Nothing more.

She folded the paper and handed it to Eddie. "You can have the invitation if you'd like."

"We're going to the open house, aren't we, Mommy?"

Kate closed her eyes and forced away the pain. "Of course. It's the neighborly thing to do."

Eddie ran off to look at the photos and Kate stayed on the couch, thinking of Luke. He didn't expect anyone to care about him or his cause. He was willing to give, give and give some more. To the animals, to Brittany, even to Kate, in a roundabout way, by paying for her help.

When she'd started working for him, she'd needed the money and he'd needed someone to ease his child into a new and stressful situation. Kate had responded to the little girl's plight, never knowing how much Brittany's life had mirrored Luke's own childhood years. Never knowing how much she'd grow to care for both father and daughter.

But as much as Kate responded to Luke's past, he was a grown man now, a man unwilling or unable to love her as she wanted to be loved. She knew she could never settle for being second or third, not after her marriage to Ed.

If she and Luke had a real relationship, they wouldn't have drifted apart so easily. If they'd been a couple, they would have talked things through. But they hadn't been a couple; they'd been two people focused on one goal.

All they'd had was friendship and great sex. Was there more, or had she imagined they were falling in love?

Chapter Sixteen

On Sunday afternoon, Kate, Eddie, Travis, Jodie and baby Marsha piled into Travis's old pickup truck and drove across the pasture. They figured there would be a big crowd from town, so there was no reason to clog Luke's driveway. They parked on the other side of the fencerow, shaded by hackberry trees, and walked the rest of the way to the "open ranch." Sure enough, it was packed with people.

"Wow, he went all out," Jodie said as they walked through an unoccupied pasture, dodging an occasional bluebonnet and staying far away from low clumps of blooming cactus. They climbed through the fence and stopped on the driveway, which was lined with cars and pickups. A large "moon walk" inflated jumping platform nearly eclipsed the house. White tents shielded tables laden with large metal urns of iced tea, plastic-wrap-covered platters of sandwiches, hot dogs, chips and pickles.

"This is bigger than the Fourth of July festival!"

Travis proclaimed, impressed despite his continued suspicion of Luke.

"He told me he was planning something big," Kate said.

"Mommy, can I go to the petting zoo?" Kate squinted at the shaded area on the other side of the house, surprised to see Cheryl Jacks's petting zoo set up for the children.

"Let's all walk over there," Jodie suggested.

They spent the next half hour walking around, greeting neighbors and friends, and sharing their amazement over the ranch. Kate pretended to observe all the changes, but she kept looking for Luke. She'd gotten a glimpse of him inside the barn, but lost him to the shade and the crowd. Then she'd seen him beside the pasture of the miniature horse, Precious, and her foal. But Brittany had pulled him away to meet her teacher, whom Kate recognized, and Kate's attention had been called away by Hank and Gwendolyn McCauley. When Kate tried to see him again, he'd disappeared.

And she became more and more irritated at herself, which she tried very hard to hide from her family.

Eddie went off with his friend Pete and Pete's parents, and Jodie and Travis stayed in conversations with Hank and Gwendolyn. "I'm going to get something cold to drink," she told them, and took off on her own.

Before she could get a soft drink and spend a few minutes alone, she saw Luke step onto the bed of his pickup. Apparently he was wired with a microphone, because suddenly he was asking for every-one's attention.

It took a few moments for the crowd to gather, the noise level to decrease enough for him to be heard. The sound of insects and birds, broken by a baby's occasional squeal of delight, suddenly seemed over-loud in the warm, sunny afternoon. Then he began to speak, words of welcome to everyone.

"This ranch is a special place for animals who had no place else to go," he said, and then told them about his dream to save the old, sick or crippled per-formance animals.

"I saw many animals put down during my time doing stunts. It's not fair, and I'm going to do my best to save as many as I can," he finished.

The crowd applauded. "I'm not asking for any donations. I have a trust fund that provides income for the upkeep of the ranch."

"But what can we do to help?" someone shouted.

Luke seemed surprised. Kate smiled as she imag-ined how he was feeling right now. Nervous, no doubt, at standing in front of a crowd of strangers. But maybe his heart would be warmed by the gener-osity of his neighbors.

Several other people shouted out offers to help, taking center stage away from Luke. He let them speak, agreeing when appropriate. When the din died down again, he continued. "I'm humbled by your of-fers. I never thought anyone would want to clean out stalls or pull weeds from fencerows," he said with a grin. The crowd laughed. He looked down for a moment, then shook his head as if clearing his thoughts. "I've been told this is a great town. You've proved my friend Hank right. And I also want to take this time to thank another friend, Kate Wooten. She helped get me and my house ready for my daughter Brittany, and I'll be eternally grateful to her and Branson Construction, and Robin Parker. Thanks, everyone!"

Once again the crowd applauded. Kate felt her cheeks heat, but not with embarrassment of being mentioned. She felt mortified that Luke was "eternally grateful" to her for her help. As if she'd performed a job, which she had. As if she wasn't any different than any other friend of his, or anyone else who had worked to get the house ready. While the attention of the crowd was still focused on Luke, she turned away, determined to flee before she had to face anyone about all her "help."

She grabbed a can of soda, then kept walking. The shady interior of the barn, where she'd watched Luke work with the ponies and do his chores, beckoned. They'd kissed there, fallen into the hay, and even quarreled. So many memories had been packed into two weeks.

She paused beside the empty stall where the little mare she'd named Precious stayed with the foal. Had Brittany named the baby yet? Had she made new friends at school? Did the commercial spoofing the Clydesdales get filmed, or was Luke still training the ponies?

In just a few weeks, Kate realized, Luke's life had become her own—not that she'd given up her own time with Eddie and her family. Then, in just a moment of passion, everything had changed. She'd made the assumption that she and Luke were even closer, but he'd seemed angry. He'd pulled away more every time she'd seen him since, and there was nothing she could do to regain the camaraderie they'd shared as they'd worked to get ready for Brittany.

"Taking a break?" Luke asked from behind her.

Kate whirled, sloshing soda over her hand. "You startled me!"

"You must have been thinking pretty hard not to hear me walk in. I wasn't trying to scare you."

Kate took a deep breath and shook the soda off her hand. "I was just looking around. Uh, did Brittany name the foal?"

Luke took the soda from her hand, placed it on a post and whipped a clean handkerchief from his pocket. Before she could protest, he took her hand in his and began to wipe her fingers. "Not yet."

She pulled her hand from his. "I should get back to Eddie." She should get out of this barn, away from Luke, and sidestep the memories of everything that had happened this past month.

"I want to talk to you, Kate."

"Why? Don't you have enough new friends?" Oh, God, that was so mean. She closed her eyes, bowed her head and ran her fingers through her hair. Her head was beginning to hurt. "I'm sorry. I don't know what's wrong with me."

"It's okay." His brow furrowed. "Are you upset because I mentioned you when I spoke earlier?"

"No, of course not," she said, trying to appear casual.

"Because I was trying to make people think that we were just friends, because some of them thought we were dating and that might upset you."

"I'm not upset!"

"You seem upset."

"Well, I'm not," she lied.

"If you were upset, I could certainly understand, because maybe I haven't handled things, like our relationship and my place in this town, too well in the past." He pulled her hands down and looked into her eyes. "Kate, you were right. Everyone has been supportive. They aren't prying into my past, just trying to get a sense of who I am. I think if I told them about my parents, they wouldn't be judgmental or try to take advantage. I didn't expect it, and I'm just glad you aren't saying, 'I told you so.'"

"I would say, 'you know me better than that,' but that's not true, is it? We really don't know each other all that well."

"I think we know the important things."

Oh, God. Why was he looking at her as though she was the most important person in the world? And why was he saying these things when he didn't mean them? At least, not the way I'm taking it, she said to herself.

"I know that you've got your hands full, settling into your role as father and taking care of your new ranch. Like you said, you've had a lot of changes in your life."

"Every one of them have been changes for the better. If I sounded like I was complaining, I didn't mean to."

"No, you weren't complaining, but I can see why you…well, why you need the support of a lot of friends." *And no one special someone.*

Luke tilted his head to the side and rubbed the back of his neck. "I have to admit, Kate, that I got a little confused about what I needed." He stepped closer, making her step back until she rested against the wooden boards of the little mare's stall.

"What do you mean?" she said, barely above a whisper.

"That I knew you were getting over your divorce—"

"Believe me, I'm well over Ed Wooten."

"Okay, then let me say you were recovering financially from what he did before the divorce."

"That's true."

"And you had a whole new life to start."

"Yes, I did. I do. I don't have any other choice. At the time it seemed like a cruel twist of fate, to have everything yanked from beneath me. Our house, Eddie's school and activities, our friends, our future. But now I see that it was the best thing that could have happened. Oh, I wish Ed hadn't done what he'd done, and that he hadn't hurt Eddie by running away, hiding from creditors and maybe even lawsuits from investors."

"I know. Eddie is a great kid. When I first met you, I didn't realize what he'd gone through. He and Brittany have a lot in common, don't they? I can see that now."

"Yes, I suppose they do. They both lost people they love and the lives they knew."

"Kind of like us. I lost my mother. You lost your marriage."

She shook her head. "I don't miss Ed at all, just the things, the life, the security, he represented."

"And I hadn't thought about my father with anything but fury in a long time. And you were right about the real source of my anger, too. I wanted to know him, or at least know a father, but since I never had that, I couldn't put it into words or even rational thought."

Kate ducked her head and smiled sadly. "I'm not a trained psychologist, but I sometimes masquerade as one when given the opportunity." She looked up at Luke. "I'm sorry that I took the liberty of confronting you on what I saw as personal issues. I didn't have the right—"

"Since, as I reminded you at the time, we were both naked, I think you had that right. I'm sorry I wasn't ready to hear it then."

Kate flushed from the memory and felt warmed by his apology. "It's okay." She looked away from his earnest expression, from the handsome face she'd grown to love in too short a time. She didn't have any self-preservation instincts when it came to men. Travis said she was naive, but Kate thought she was just too susceptible to Luke.

He tipped her chin with his hand. "The thing is, Kate, that it's only okay if we're ready *now*."

"What do you mean?"

"That I'm ready to move forward, not dwell on the past. And I want to move forward with you. And Eddie and Brittany, of course."

"I don't understand what you mean."

He suddenly pulled her close, hugged her tightly and rested his chin on the top of her head. "I'm not saying this well, am I? I want to be with you, Kate, every day and every week. Not just the two we spent together, which were two of the best weeks in my whole life, I might add. I don't know much about family. I never had a father, and my mother and I were all the family we had. I've never had a home before now. But now I have a daughter and a place I love, and I want to share it with you and your son."

Kate pulled back in his arms and looked at Luke. "You do?"

He grinned. "I do."

She blushed when she realized what they'd just said.

"I know you need time to get used to me. And Brittany. And maybe even the idea of committing yourself to us. I'm willing to give you time, Kate, as much as you need. Just don't give up on me. On us."

"I never stopped thinking you were a very special

man. And I told you that you'd be a wonderful father, didn't I?"

"Well, yeah. But that doesn't mean I have what it takes to form a family. I understand if you're a little cautious—"

"I've been—or tried to be—a cautious person all my life. But Luke, I don't need time to get used to you. Don't you know that you're in my thoughts all the time? Don't you know that I wonder about you and Brittany, about how you're getting along. What she's doing each day? I'm so used to you that I was angry with myself for loving a man who couldn't love me back."

Luke's body went tense and he gripped her tightly. "You love me?"

"Of course I love you," she said, tears forming as she gazed into his surprised face. "How could I not love a man whose goal in life is to provide a ranch for homeless animals, who embraces the idea of his eight-year-old child, who loved his mother and yearned for his father all these years? How could I not love a man who has so much to give, but at the same time, expects so little from everyone else around him?" She framed his face with her hands and whispered, "I love you, Luke Simon, for the man you are today. And I respect you for the way you got to where you are today. And if you're asking me if we have a future, then my answer is yes."

His expression changed from wonder to love as he looked down at her, then he pulled her close and kissed her, the kiss of a man in love, the kiss of someone who believed in forever. She responded, clung to him, kissed him with all that was in her, until they were both winded and aroused and still in wonder.

"Isn't there something you forgot to tell me?" she asked, breathing heavily as she leaned back enough to see his face.

He frowned. "I think I told you all the family secrets."

"There's nothing else that you haven't said?"

She could see his mind working, going over their conversation, maybe even their entire relationship. Then he started to smile, and his body relaxed against hers.

"Yeah, there's something. One little thing," he said with a grin. "I love you, Kate Wooten, with all my heart."

She smiled back. "That's all I needed to hear." She leaned up and kissed him again. This time, when they came up for air, she added, "And the answer is yes."

Epilogue

"I can't believe you're here at the Fourth of July parade with your wedding just days away," Jodie said to Kate as they stood in the dappled shade of the crepe myrtles, near the gazebo. The air was hot and dry, the wind still.

"I wouldn't miss it for the world," Kate replied, standing on tiptoes and straining to see past the next car, filled with smiling and waving young beauty queens. "I think they're marching soon."

"Brittany has sure blossomed under your care," Jodie observed, repositioning Marsha on her hip.

"She needed a home."

"She got a home and a family."

Kate grinned at her sister-in-law. "We all did." Everyone she knew in Rangers Springs, from Robin and Ethan Parker to Hank and Gwendolyn, had made her feel welcome in her new hometown. Even the couples she barely knew, like the former Kerry Jacks who was now a princess, and her husband, Prince Alexi, along with their two children, had made her feel a part of the extended family. Charlene Jacks had married the handsome contractor who'd remodeled Luke's house. Luke had mentioned having Nate add on to their house, since they wanted more room for those "dozen or so children" Luke promised her.

Kate smiled to herself. One or two more would do. Probably. She loved children. She'd love teaching second grade next month, right after their wedding at the church here in town, their reception at Bretford House, and honeymoon in Banff, Canada, while everyone in town pitched in to care for the ranch.

A sleek convertible rolled by, driven by Gray Phillips. Dr. Amy was seated in the front, the seat belt stretched around her large middle. Jodie had told Kate that the family practitioner was due in September, finally becoming pregnant after seeing so many of her friends and neighbors have children. Joyce and Ranger Springs mayor Ambrose Wheatley sat on the top of the back seat, waving enthusiastically at the crowd. He was up for reelection this fall, and chances were he'd run unopposed.

A customized vintage Camaro, emblazoned with the Ranger Springs Police Department emblem, rolled by, driven by a handsome officer Kate didn't recognize. "Who's that?" she asked Jodie.

"Travis said that's Rick Alvarado. He left Ranger Springs a couple of years ago for a job with the feds, but came back recently. Talk around the square is that he returned because of Gina Mae Summers."

"The real estate lady?"

"Word is that they'll be looking for a cozy house in town real soon."

Kate's smile widened as Gwendolyn walked up, carrying her son. "Hank will be riding by soon. I want to get some photos."

"Me, too." Kate's camera dangled from her wrist as she watched for the next marching group. There! Just past the convertible, Luke came into sight, leading two of the new ponies he'd trained for the children. The flashy pintos had been found by Charlene's middle daughter, Cheryl, when she was out with her petting zoo. They'd been undernourished and living without shelter from the sun, so she'd browbeat the owner into turning them over to her. She'd presented them to Luke, who'd soon determined they were perfect for Brittany and Eddie.

"Is Cheryl Jacks participating today?" Kate had heard she usually had her petting zoo available for the children on the square, but she hadn't seen the pens today.

"Haven't you heard? She ran off and got married yesterday."

"No way!" Kate exclaimed.

"To whom?" Gwendolyn asked.

"Her sister Carole's brother-in-law, Brad Rafferty."

"She married her brother-in-law?"

"Well, he's not Cheryl's brother-in-law. He's Carole's husband Greg's brother," Jodie explained.

Kate shook her head. "That's going to be very confusing if they ever have children."

"I'm sure they'll get it straightened out in time to tell Carole and Greg's toddler."

"Carole's daughter Jennifer will probably take charge."

The conversation had distracted her, but Kate waved at her husband-to-be and children as they passed. She now thought of Brittany as hers even though the adoption wouldn't go through until after the wedding. Luke also wanted to adopt Eddie, and since Ed had no interest in his son now that he was ruined financially, she didn't think that would be a problem.

She snapped some photos of her family, and then the animals that followed, led by local 4-H teen volunteers: Lola and Lollipop, the zebras; the two white horses outfitted in fancy bridles with plumes; and finally, Jennifer's pet steer, Puff, who wore a banner promising "Miss Carole's cookies for everyone after the parade." Back at the Last Chance Ranch, a flock of emus—courtesy of Chief Ethan Parker, who'd found the birds blocking the country road for the umpteenth time, he said—and many other new animals grazed and nibbled and slept in the shade, all as happy as Kate to find a place to call home.

Brittany and Eddie perched proudly on their ponies, dressed in cowboy outfits designed and sewn by Helen Kaminsky, Travis and Jodie's housekeeper. At that moment, surrounded by friends and family, in the midst of her adopted community, Kate felt as if she were the luckiest woman in the world.

She'd thought she had everything she wanted be-

fore, with a successful husband, a house in the suburbs and enough money to spend on luxuries. Now
she knew true happiness came from within, from
being content with herself and loved by a good man.
From raising children who needed her and friends
who liked her, and from giving to the community
through teaching and other activities.

She was one lucky woman, she thought, throwing
a kiss at her handsome fiancé. She would have never
called her divorce and the loss of everything material
as "luck," but she'd landed here in Ranger Springs and
found the love of her life and the family of her dreams.

Yes, she was one lucky woman, she thought with
a smile, raising the camera and taking one more photo
so she would remember today for the rest of her life.

American **ROMANCE®**

Motherhood

**Motherhood: what it
means to raise a child.**

THE BABY
INHERITANCE
by **Ann Roth**
American Romance #1103

When Mia Barker learns she has been named
legal guardian of a relative's baby, she finds
herself in a state of shock. Running a vet clinic
and taking care of animals is one thing, but with
a painful event from her past still haunting her,
she doesn't feel capable of raising a child. Can
Hank Adams convince Mia to let baby
Drew—and him—into her heart?

*Available February 2006
wherever Harlequin books are sold.*

SHOWCASING...

New York Times bestselling author

JOAN HOHL

HOME TO LOVE

**A classic story about two people
who finally discover great love....**

"Ms. Hohl always creates a vibrant ambiance
to capture our fancy."
—*Romantic Times*

Coming in February.

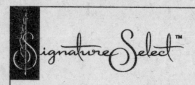

Signature Select™

And the envelope, Please...

Three brand-new awards-season stories by

USA TODAY bestselling author
BARBARA BRETTON
and
EMILIE ROSE
ISABEL SHARPE

Three couples find romance on the red carpet at
the glamorous Reel New York Awards—where
the A-list rules and passion and egos collide!

*Look for this fun and lighthearted collection
in February 2006!*

A breathtaking novel of
reunion and romance…

THE F⬧RTUNES OF TEXAS™: *Reunion*

Once a Rebel

by **Sheri WhiteFeather**

Returning home to Red Rock after many
years, psychologist Susan Fortune is reunited
with Ethan Eldridge, a man she hasn't gotten
over in seventeen years. When tragedy and grief
overtake the family, Susan leans on Ethan to
overcome her feelings—and soon realizes that
her life can't be complete without him.

Coming in February

Silhouette®
Where love comes alive™

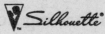

SPECIAL EDITION™

HUSBANDS AND OTHER STRANGERS

by
Marie Ferrarella

A boating accident left Gayle Elliott Conway with amnesia and no recollection of the handsome man who came to her rescue…her husband. Convinced there was more to the story, Taylor Conway set out for answers and a way back into the heart of the woman he loved.

Available February 2006